# Coyote Crossing

## Phil Baechler

# Coyote Crossing

### By
### Phil Baechler

*'Los coyotes corren; en el día, en la noche. Mira —
allí estan:
corriendo, siempre corriendo...'*

\*\*\*\*

# Coyote Crossing

## By
## Phil Baechler

Javelina Press First Print Edition

©2016 Phil Baechler

****

For the desert.

# Chapter One

Raging flash flood waters from the Arizona monsoon thunderstorms aboveground swirled violently as they drained through the Grand Tunnel buried deep below Nogales, Arizona. Or it could still be Nogales, Sonora, if they hadn't waded under the border yet. The water swirled around Tina's knees, much deeper than she had expected. She inched forward through the dark tunnel, counting every step.

Slips and stumbles in the mud counted as half steps and they were rapidly adding up. She and Blanco's grandmother Luz had waded close to a mile now through the darkness. Where was the rest of her group? Tina had stayed behind to help the struggling Luz as the others disappeared into the darkness ahead.

Tina's flashlight had quit working after the third dunking, and her hand was getting tired from Luz' clinging grip. The old woman had slipped and pulled her under the muck close to a dozen times by now, leaving her gritty and spitting fishy-tasting slime. Luz had lost her flashlight on the first tumble.

Tina was almost positive they had crossed the invisible line that separated Mexico from the gringo side. Several groups of "coyotes" who had led their refugee bands through the huge culverts in the past few days had destroyed the lights, sirens and any other deterrents the American *Migra* had put up along the subterranean gauntlet. *El Grande* was just that: a tunnel big enough to drive a Humvee through…if its engine could run underwater without stalling in the torrent that poured through the underground culverts from the late summer rainstorms.

Tina slid her right hand along the slippery wall, her back scraping the wet cement, her left hand gripping Luz' clinging fingers. Ahead, a couple dozen compatriots had left them behind and vanished through the maze of culverts, drainage lids and vents that led aboveground to American soil. José had been the point man, the lead coyote guide charged with getting this flock of *cruzeros* to the waiting van or pickup truck that would take them to a safe house where they would hide out before the next leg of the trip north. Tina had been carrying the "greenback pack," stuffed with half a million dollars to guarantee safe passage north for Antonio Blanco and his family. That was a lot of cash, but Blanco was a big fish in the Colombian cartels, moving north before a bullet caught up with him. When Blanco's mother Luz had begun to struggle, Tina had passed the bag to José and stayed behind with her.

"*Casi alli*", she told Luz. Almost there, although it was impossible to tell in the darkness, their flashlights swept away after one of the many slips on the slippery bottom, made even more treacherous by the currents sweeping in from all directions through side tunnels. At least the muddy water had diluted the sewage that usually trickled through the system, making the smell tolerable. The maze of pipes under the border crossing between Mexico and the U.S. was more than a century old and virtually impossible to police. Drugs, immigrants all followed the same trail the Spaniards followed north: the tide of waters that created the Santa Cruz River as it flowed into the Gila. You can't stop Mother Nature, Tina thought.

At every vortex that marked a discharge from the side tunnels, she waited, ears keened for the border agents — *la Migra* — that often hid in the side passages to capture *cruzeros* — the border crossers. Members of the Border Patrol. *My erstwhile co-workers.* If some of them could see me now: underground, under cover, under water…tracking a killer among them.

But that was the last thing she wanted to happen. This was working "internal affairs" at its worst, swamping her way through a sewage drain to infiltrate the gangs that ran the corrupt billion dollar smuggling traffic in drugs, desperate job seekers, and worse, weapons of terror. Somewhere in that viper's nest, her predecessor had been murdered. For many reasons, Tina had a score to settle, so that made it personal.

Luz slipped, pulling her under. Tina's leg scraped across a shard of metal from a gate torn apart by monsoon currents. They were definitely in Arizona now — every year the Americans rebuilt the metal grating only to have the debris-laden storm waters knock it down. She fought to keep her head above water, struggled to pull Luz back to a shallower part of the drainage. This was supposed to be Tina's big chance: help José get the batch of *cruzeros* across to prove herself, move up the pecking order and into the next level of trust—a narco crossing and eventually into the cartel's inner circle where the money men called the shots.

It had become a billion dollar business, relatives in Phoenix willing to shell out more than $1000 apiece for safe arrival of their loved ones. The cash on delivery was a new trend, intended to keep the *cruzeros* from becoming easy targets for robbers on their way north. The downside was that rival coyotes, or *polleros* in Spanish, now hijacked entire truckloads of illegals at gunpoint, often with fatal results.

Tina hated the irony of the United States' enforcement efforts. How dare these people want to mow our lawns and clean our kitchens? But policy wasn't her job. Enforcement was. It was often dangerous; make that always dangerous when you were working incognito alongside murderous thugs.

Just as she got Luz pulled over closer to the edge, the culvert bottom dropped off at a steep angle and pitched them into a cavernous catch basin. Tina remembered this junction from the map of the culvert complex. They had to bear right to get to stay in the storm drainage and avoid being swept to the left and ending up in the sewage system.

She pulled on Luz's arm: "*Derecha! Vamos a la derecha!*"

Other shouts followed hers: "*Parate! Migra! Manos arriba!*" The orders and sudden lights came from their right.

*Shit.*

Luz broke free from Tina's grip, tried to turn up-current, but tumbled back and was yanked onto a maintenance ledge along the tunnel wall by one of the uniformed figures emerging from the gloom. Luz screamed and Tina reached for her, but instead felt her own arm wrenched as dark uniforms pulled them into a side channel. Pushed them forward around a bend. Lights from aboveground blinded them now and they were pushed up the metal rungs of a ladder, through a drainage grate and onto a sandy ditch bank.

"Those other dipshits shouldn't have been so worried about *los mujeres*," one of the agents laughed. "If they'd kept their mouths shut, these twats probably would have washed downstream all the way to the pecan orchards and got away."

Tina swallowed her anger, forcing herself to ignore the crude English that she *shouldn't* be able to understand. As far as these assholes were concerned, she was Valentina Corazón from Quetzaltenango, Guatemala.

Above the banking Tina could see the roof of a Border Patrol bus lit by the glare of portable spotlights. Standard operating procedure. Movable checkpoints, every night and day — a constantly shifting maze of checkpoints and personnel. Someplace in that maze lurked a killer in uniform and it was Tina's job to track him.

Luz was covered in mud, the left leg of her pants torn, her white hair brown with dirt. Tina, stronger, more alert, helped steer Luz along, giving no hint that she understood the English being shouted at them as they were herded up the ridge to the bus, its windows blacked out by reflective panels.

"*Andales, mujeres* — stand over here by the bus." Luz was shivering now and Tina put her arms over her shoulders. There were two Border Patrol agents with them now, and one stood guard with a shotgun while the other bound their hands in front of them with plastic handcuff ties. Standard operating procedure.

Then the agent who had finished binding their wrists pulled off his helmet and Tina had to fight back a gasp of recognition. The redheaded bastard! She was sure it was him, but the last time she had seen him it had been months before and through binoculars.

He came closer, looking at her, then across to Luz, then back at her. Taking a glance over his shoulder he called out to his partner: "This scrawny old one ain't much to look at, but I sure wouldn't mind getting my hands on this tall Aztec-looking bitch."

As he turned back to her with a leer, Tina fought back any recognition that she understood what he was saying. Spanish, she was only supposed to know Spanish. "*Su nombre, mujer?*" Coming closer, his red hair looked strangely orange in the halogen glare. She wouldn't need to know English to understand his body language — her cringe spoke for itself. "Maybe I better check her for identification."

His eyes were riveted on her breasts, outlined starkly by her clinging, damp blouse and the harsh lights.

Tina looked away from him and, in Spanish, warned Luz: "Whatever happens, try to go home. Get out of here. Go back to Guatemala or Colombia. Don't trust the *polleros* again. *Comprende?*"

Luz nodded numbly, water from her hair dripping into her eyes. Tina looked back to the redhead as he finished "frisking" her front pants pockets, ignoring the passport stuffed there, and started working his fingertips up her ribs, under the round weight of her breasts, up the center seam of her blouse. As his eyes joined his fingertips on the top button, Tina struck like a sidewinder, pounding her forehead into his nose. A shotgun blast ripped the night, over their heads, but a few pellets rattled the edge of the bus roof.

"Bitch!" the redhead screamed, his left hand going to his nose, the right swinging around against the side of Tina's head, sending her spinning toward the dirt and darkness.

"What the hell's going on back here?" Footsteps, a rush of voices, pushing, "Quit dickin' around and get them loaded on the bus!"

Tina floated, battling the current again, swimming against the black tide of unconsciousness as she felt herself dumped into a seat on the bus. Luz was a couple of rows ahead, looking back with a mixture of fear and concern. An older woman sat beside Tina, looking sadly at the plastic binding her own wrists. As Tina gave up fighting to stay awake, the redheaded bastard floated into her memory, back at the border in Naco when it all began... was it the same guy?

****

# Chapter Two

It had started the previous spring — prime smuggling season as fruit, vegetables and lettuce from Mexico rolled northward by the truckload — in Naco, Arizona, the epitome of what news reports would call a "dusty border town." A flurry of interest would occasionally blow through when the neo-Nazi "militias" did their sporadic charade of "border protection," drug murders in Mexico hit double digits, or, worse, a U.S. agent was killed near the "fence." On that late spring afternoon, Tina had perched in a second floor bedroom, peering through the curtain slats at the 1930s-era Santa Fe style border station two blocks away. The antique building that housed the Port of Entry, with its flat roof and wooden beams protruding from the stucco façade, could have passed for a parody of a drive-thru taco stand were it not for the coiled razor wire fence on either side and the rotating pedestrian gate in the walkway. Occasional Americans heading south in their motor homes rumbled over the grade crossing to follow the Rio Sonora road to Hermosillo.

They got hardly a glance on the Mexican side: vehicle, insurance and identity papers wouldn't be checked until they got a couple dozen miles down the highway south of Nogales.Tina got up from her chair, stretched, rubbed her eyes to relieve the strain of peering through the binoculars. The floor creaked underneath her. The ancient stucco-over-frame house that served as the surveillance point would have turned to paper maché in a wetter climate. It was no beauty, but the window looked out past an alley and over a boarded-up trailer straight at the border crossing. Downstairs, the rickety garage door shielded her gleaming new 1999 BMW R1100S motorcycle from prying eyes.

She looked over at her dark purple motorcycle helmet and the leather jacket on the side of the unused bed, next to the telephone on the nightstand. Tonight, the crossing was supposed to be tonight. The code had come yesterday to the control center in Tucson. Tina didn't know who had sent the message from across the border, or how it had been delivered. That wasn't her job.

She went back to the window and continued her surveillance. The code had been specific: Mixed into the alpha-numeric camouflage were the key symbols — "T-D-N"…it would be a truck, crossing at either Douglas or Naco.

Would the crossing be here? This was the hard part, the waiting. She had drawn the shift at Naco, an undercover agent watching sworn law enforcement officers of her own government. Who watches the watchers?

In this case, two Border Patrol agents staffed the truck crossing. One had a German Shepherd on a leash.

It made sense for smugglers to target the smaller stations at Naco and Douglas. With all the contentiousness about border issues, increased enforcement in California and Texas had pushed much of the illegal traffic to Arizona.

The crossing at Nogales was huge, more than a thousand trucks a day rolling through the latest in high-tech screening, a regular showcase of tax dollars at work. That left the quieter ports at Naco and Douglas as the easiest holes in the sieve. A van with a mom and two kids rolled up to the border, the woman waving to one of the gate agents. He looked at his partner, who was standing in the middle of the single lane holding the dog's leash. The dog handler gave a short nod. The woman slid into the passenger seat as her husband hopped in, fastened his seat belt and made a deft U-turn. Shift change. Tina was on alert, sensing the thin staffing and fading light. The remaining agent walked the dog over to the corner of the building and looped its leash over a faucet handle. The dog lapped some water from the bowl under the faucet, then plopped down against the stucco wall and looked at his handler, who pulled a cell phone out of a back pocket and punched a dial preset. Tina adjusted the focus on her binoculars but couldn't make out what he was saying. As a linguist, she had learned to read lips as a hobby. Having grown up bouncing back and forth between her father's office in Washington, DC, his law firm in Phoenix and their ancestral homeland on the Navajo reservation, she had had no shortage of subjects to practice on. Her mother, Michelle, would make it a game at embassy parties, whispering to her in Vietnamese to guess where a particular person was from just by watching their lips move. The phone slipped back into the agent's pocket and he stepped into the guard shack and tapped a few keys on the computer. Just then, she heard the rumble of a semi rolling up from the right. She lowered the binoculars. Even from this distance she could see the cornucopia of tomatoes, fruit and vegetables painted on the side of the trailer. She also heard the first "beep" from the earpiece in her helmet. This was it. Whoever had sent the coded message had also planted a radio transmitter someplace on the truck. Tina's job was to track it.She focused on the cab. The driver handed a clipboard down to the agent, his dark

16

blue uniform almost black in the fading light. The agent flipped a couple pages, looked up at the driver, gave him back the clipboard, waved him through. As the truck pulled away, the agent stuffed something into his back pocket. Tina knew it wasn't the phone. Bastard, she thought. The dog was too far away to smell anything on the truck, no paperwork had been left behind, and as the semi rolled slowly away up the hill toward Bisbee, Tina saw two cars roll into the parking lot with the night shift agents. She turned away from the window, grabbed the phone on the nightstand and punched in a code that would signal over the secure landline that she had made contact. She would be keeping radio silence on this trip — unless it was a "Mayday." Too many signals had been intercepted lately. Trust was in short supply. She slipped into the motorcycle jacket and zipped it up — a custom tailored Vanson that gave her torso what aerodynamics could be afforded via tucks and zippers. The leather was a purple so dark as to look black, especially at night. The pants matched and she was all business tonight — the chaps and vest for summer riding were stashed in her apartment in Tucson waiting for her next "recreational" ride. Lady linguist in leather…what the heck, she liked a little alliteration. She piled her shoulder length black hair on top of her head, stretched an elastic around it, buckled her helmet and slipped on her gloves as she took the stairs two at a time down to the garage. The BMW fired right up and Tina let it warm in the driveway while she locked the garage behind her. Chances are she'd never be back, and there was nothing in the house worth stealing, but the house was "safe" and would be ready for the next ops person who needed it. As she swung her leg over the BMW, she patted the slim, extremely sharp knife tucked into her boot. She had carried it in her Burkha during her first undercover mission: Kuwait, Desert Storm. Guns had come and gone, but she had always kept the knife. Great-Grandfather Victor Toledo had made it in the shop aboard ship when he served as a Code Talker in World War II. The story that had passed with the knife down the generations told of a Kamikaze plane that had hit their ship, and that after the fire was put out, Great-Grandfather had found a stub of samurai sword twisted in the rubble. Tina could still see a Japanese character on the blade whenever she sharpened it. As she rolled up to the corner and made the turn toward the border station, she found herself wondering for the first time if she was getting too old for this "Jane Bond" stuff. She'd be 33 as the century rolled over on the odometer.

She accelerated up the street toward the border station and checked the GPS screen on her handlebars. The locator blip from the truck blinked slowly on the map, about two miles up the road, about the effective range of the tracking beacon. It wasn't going to outrun her BMW. She had nicknamed it Black Eagle, and it could fly: 150 horsepower, with a fairing and windscreen for high-speed touring, yet enough suspension travel to survive the desert detours that seemed to come with the job. The twin panniers in back packed enough gear to survive a week, including her standard issue SIG P228. The pistol was ready, and she was an expert shot, but in her more than a decade-and-a-half of military and government service she had yet to shoot anyone. The knife, though, had been a silent friend on a couple of occasions. The memories were there, but she didn't dwell on them. In a way it was an irony: Words and their camouflage had been at the root of her family's heritage as Code Talkers. Her great-grandfather Victor Toledo and grandfather Nez had both joined the Marines and served together under Admiral Nimitz. Words and their minute shadings had led to her father Chester Toledo's career as a lawyer and diplomat, after his tour as a Marine in Vietnam. Mama Michelle had been a girl of 17 working as a translator in the U.S. embassy in Saigon when Papa met her. Words had led Tina into cryptology and military intelligence, the Marines and Kuwait. She knew names in more than twenty languages for just about everything, had named her motorcycle Black Eagle, and yet the knife was simply…the knife.

# Chapter Three

The window frame thumped Tina awake as the busload of prisoners went over a bump.

*"Esta bien?"* the woman to her left asked. Tina felt the forehead over her left eye: tender and swollen, but she could see. She hoped the redhead bastard's nose was thoroughly broken. The bus looked full to her. The seven members of the Blanco family had been part of a group of 30 that José and she had started with. Other seats were filled with tired looking faces she didn't recognize.

The movement of the bus was making Tina a little dizzy, but she forced a smile.

*"Yo vivo,"* she told her seatmate, making sure to use the slightly thick-sounding tongue she had picked up in Guatemala. She knew it would sound authentic: Grandmother Estrella had insisted on adding Spanish and the Tohono O'odham dialect to the family's native Navajo. Fascinated by the many species of words, much like some people become ornithologists, Tina grew up as a "wordwatcher" instead of a birdwatcher. She had collected her own Native American Athapascan, Hopic and Uto-Aztecan dialects of Navajo, Apache, Yaqui, Hopi and the Tohono O'odham of her grandmother's scattered people, as well as the Spanish of grandmother Estrella's padre Seferino.

From her mother Michelle had come French and Vietnamese. And from her father Chester, ever the attorney and diplomat, precise English, which she increasing found to be the most inscrutable of all, a treacherous tongue subject to manipulation, obfuscation and shading. A language made for liars.

In addition to speaking, she'd learned to listen, both to the words and to the accent and inflection. Not to mention the silences. She'd learned in Kuwait that silence from a woman was not unexpected. Silence aided invisibility. Survival depended on it.

Tina reached over and squeezed the woman's hand, *"Yo vivo."*

She closed her eyes, leaned against the bus window and tried to picture the redhead again—tonight in Nogales. Had it been the same guy she had seen waving the truck through the border checkpoint months ago in Naco? She couldn't be sure. Through the binoculars, she had been watching the whole scene, not yet aware of who the players would be. Then, the truck had gotten the "free pass" across the border and she had launched Black Eagle and set off in pursuit. The only clear glimpse of the redhead had been through the window of the guard shack as she had rolled out of Naco after the truck…

**\*\*\*\***

…Up the ridge to Bisbee, keeping the semi in range on the GPS screen. Tina knew the Eagle would have no trouble chasing the truck and that the radio transmitter planted on it would be good for at least 48 hours, but she wanted to stay close enough for visual contact in case it made any stops or picked up passengers. She toggled the control button on her left handlebar and watched her monitor's dropdown screen that showed the listing of radio frequencies available for scanning. The wireless headphones in her helmet were quiet so far. She would be listening for clues in the ether around the truck as well as tracking its movements. All systems go. The last item she checked was her own locator beacon. Now that she was moving, she used the touch screen on the control panel and set it to "ping" every 15 minutes: a tiny blip that would tell the control center where she was. Funny, she had no idea where the control center was actually located. All she had to know was to stick with the truck. She caught up with the semi as it downshifted to crawl toward the top of the grade going into Bisbee. She intended to catch it as it dropped into the roundabout, a circular traffic loop in a huge mile-wide bowl atop the ridge. The bowl was emblematic of the rocky scars left by a century of copper mining.  The whole landscape was spiky, jagged rocks blasted by dynamite and unsoftened by time, erosion and the lush vegetation that thrived elsewhere in the Sonoran highland. Tina had always loved this part of the desert. The shrubbery and cacti, especially the noble Saguaros reaching toward the sky, were a Garden of Eden compared to the windswept Navajoland. She crested the ridge and spotted the truck entering the loop below, rocky roads spiraling out in four directions. She pictured years of ore trucks hauling tons of rocks through the merry-go-round, ant-like drones to the scoop shovels that dug the Lavender Pit deep into the earth. She turned right at the top of the bowl and looked down at the circle as the semi curved west. As it approached the turnoff to Bisbee, she rolled down the grade toward the roundabout, but when she reached the bottom of

the grade, she spotted the truck continuing around the circle
back towards her. Shit, was Vegetable Man making a whole
loop…checking to see if he was being followed? She was
already turning into the circle, so she goosed the throttle,
stayed ahead of the truck, took the first exit from the
roundabout straight up the hill toward the east. Back at
plateau level, she rolled past a scattering of classic houses that
used to hold mine workers but were now in big demand from
retirees. Along the north side of the highway she pulled into
somebody's nostalgic dream: An antique trailer court with
classic Airstream campers clustered around a 1950s replica
diner. It was so last century, but history was a big hook for
tourists in this part of Arizona. She checked the locator screen,
verified the semi had indeed made a double loop and
continued into Bisbee. She turned the BMW around and set
out in pursuit. Through the roundabout she resisted the
temptation to lean the bike over and goose the throttle for a
high-G loop. The truck driver's unpredictable maneuver had
her on edge. Nothing but business tonight. The turnoff to the
"historic" section of Bisbee cut under an ancient railroad
bridge and opened into a granite valley bordered by the huge
pit of the copper mine on the left. She could see the truck just
ahead, climbing another grade up out of town. The sun was
on the horizon ahead and darkness filled the Lavender Pit.
Deep it was, she couldn't recall how deep, but she had looked
over the edge many times to the foul water that accumulated
at the bottom. The first time she had stopped, on a "girl trip"
with some old high school friends from Phoenix when she
was on summer break later from studying at Annapolis, she
had bought a chunk of Bisbee Blue turquoise to take back to
her Grandfather Nez. Now the lights that made the sides of
the pit glow blue and green at night were clicking on, but she
sped past beauty, hardly glanced at the old downtown lined
with ornate brick buildings left from the boom days of gold
and copper. The highway crawled underground through a
quarter mile long tunnel out of the valley, and Tina rolled out

into the plains that stretched for miles, lit with the fading orange glow trapped in scattered clouds. She drove up close enough behind the truck to see that one of the running lights on the top of the trailer was burned out, giving it a gap-toothed look like a row of corn with a kernel missing. That also meant the driver could see her. If he had, in fact, been expecting a tail, he may have taken note of her and the motorcycle back at the roundabout. Tina decided the best thing to do was to hide in plain sight by disappearing in front of him. Visibility was forever in the clear night air, so she goosed the BMW up to 100 mph and flashed her lights as she blew by him. She hit 120 as the truck's lights shrank to a speck in her mirrors. She eased off the throttle, alert but tense. Night was closing in now, but her day was just starting. *Hozho*, stay focused. Five miles later, the road crested a slight rise and she spotted a ranch road that disappeared into a brushy arroyo. Tina pulled off the highway, killed her lights and spun a U-turn behind a huge mesquite. She flipped up her visor, pulled the binoculars from the left pannier, and watched the truck roll past, followed by a Mercedes that was close, waiting for a place to pass. She waited for two more cars to go by, then got in the saddle and pulled back onto the highway behind a van. The running lights of the semi were faintly visible ahead and she counted on the van to shield her single headlight. The tracker target was right on the edge of her screen. Okay, just enough leash.

There was a fork a few miles ahead and Tina knew Vegetable Man could either continue straight on through Tombstone to Benson and the Interstate, or turn left toward Sierra Vista and the army post at Fort Huachuca. She was betting on the Interstate.

She guessed wrong. As she rolled past the sign marking the junction, she saw the semi swinging left, bypassing the straight shot to Interstate 10. Had he been radioed a warning about one of the roving customs checkpoints set up south of Tombstone to collect traffic from both Douglas and Naco? It was entirely possible he had been warned. The smugglers had gotten extremely sophisticated with their own communications and, worse, at tapping into what U.S. authorities were doing. Hence Tina's radio silence, both receiving and transmitting. Secure communication was vital. Great-Grandfather Victor Toledo and Grandfather Nez had proven that among the Code Talkers of WWII. Tina had no idea as to where the enforcement checkpoint was set up tonight, but this road wasn't a direct route to anywhere. Complicating matters, the other cars behind the truck had all continued north, so she would be forced to drop back and play cat and mouse to stay out of sight in the truck's mirrors. She eased off on Black Eagle's throttle, kept an eye in her mirror for another car or van to help screen her, saw none, finally settled into a rhythm up and over the rolling terrain. The truck's running lights with the blank spot were clearly visible and there was absolutely no other traffic out here, so she switched off her headlight and flew west through the darkness. The screen on her handlebars glowed blue and she scrolled through the functions as the highway divider lines flashed by rhythmically on the left edge of her visor. When the setting for the ping came up, she reset it to ten-minute intervals, smiling with a touch of pride as she remembered writing that particular algorithm herself.

The electronics stuffed into her fairing would power a small office and had cost more than the bike itself. Tina had bought the BMW, but had the U.S. taxpayers to thank for the navigation and communications gear that snaked through the streamlined pod tipped by the darkened headlight.

A dozen miles and up ahead she saw the glow of Sierra Vista and the blinking light of the airfield at Fort Huachuca. She'd actually had a training assignment at the Army post, the latest in electronic surveillance and targeting, before shipping out to Kuwait. She'd gotten plenty of ribbing during the classes, ostensibly because she was a Marine, nothing to do with gender, of course. She'd nodded and kept her mouth shut, but had let her quickness speak during the hand-to-hand combat refresher.

That assignment was also when she wrote the ping program and helped the electronic techs stuff together a small surprise package she had personally delivered for Saddam Hussein. About the size of poker chip, each beacon would chirp on a rotating frequency every thirty seconds for about 48 hours, sending an electronic "kick me" signal to the smart bombs that had headlined the evening news as they rained down on Kuwait from the F-14 Tomcats. Even smart bombs could use a little help. Tina's favorite flourishing touch to the design had been the two-sided color scheme of the casing, giving her a range of sand tones that helped the discs blend in wherever she stuck them during her clandestine strolls through Kuwait City. Vegetable Man's truck had started slowing down as it approached town, so Tina pulled over to the roadside and let its gap grow. Radio from the air traffic control at the army post was audible so she blocked that frequency, setting the receiver to scan only for police band, CB and direct transmission inside the tight radius she was keeping on her quarry. Lights back on, she tweaked Black Eagle's throttle and closed the gap on the semi, relieved to blend in with the traffic from the scattered tract housing and trailer parks that seemed to be the modern camp followers of every military base she'd seen. Four lanes now, and she idled slowly, ignoring another motorcyclist who came alongside, gunned his Harley, then accelerated away when she gave no sign of wanting to play.

The road curved north through strip malls, fast food and pawnshops. As "civilization" thinned, she could see her the semi up ahead, turning right into a truck stop. What the heck was this? A stop was totally off any script she could have anticipated. Diesel was cheap in Mexico, so fuel couldn't be an issue. Aside from the broken light, the truck looked and sounded brand new. It had to be a planned stop — she just didn't know the plan.

Half a block up on the left was a taco joint and a mini-mart with a pay phone. Tina parked on the back side, the motorcycle out of view from the truck stop. Putting her helmet over the GPS screen, she pulled a remote earphone out of a zippered pocket on her jacket and tucked it into her left ear. She grabbed her helmet, picked up a car/truck tabloid from the "free" rack outside the door, went in and ordered a small *horchata,* sat looking out the window over the newspaper propped against her helmet.

She savored the rich cinnamon of the *horchata* — it was good, not too sweet — and tried to figure out what was going on with her prey. The semi had pulled close to another truck in the diagonal pull-throughs, the broken running light above Vegetable Man's rear door clearly visible, but the rest of the trailer hiding behind the other rig. The girl at the taco counter had her back to the dining area, chatting with the kid in the food prep area. Tina took another sip, turned the pages of the usual "Must Sell!" motor home and camper ads, and spotted another vehicle joining the party across the street.

It was an SUV, looked like an Expedition, but this was no soccer mom, boat-towing rig with dressy chrome. It was black, and not shiny, either. The big tires weren't for show and had the mud to prove it. A couple of serious looking radio antennas perched on the roof alongside a light bar. As it pulled around the two semis, Tina failed to spot a license and was out of her chair, dumping the empty cup and crumpled newspaper in the bin on her way out the door, holding it open for an older couple coming in from the parking lot.

She pulled her helmet on and grabbed the binoculars. Slipping behind the taco place, her black leather blended into an overgrown hedge of oleanders. She quickly noted the licenses of the two semis into memory, but all she could see of the SUV was one tire under the front of the cabs. It had pulled around in front of the two bigger trucks, out of the line of sight from the rest of the truck stop. She refocused the binoculars at ground level under the trucks: nothing but feet, two pair with jeans and scuffed cowboy boots. The third pair looked like combat boots and desert camouflage fatigues, but in the dark it was hard to be sure. If it was camo, it was working up to design specs.

The feet scattered and one pair came around and climbed into the front truck. The SUV rolled away, as did the truck in front. *Not my truck.*

The truck in front had obscured the one she was following, which now rolled through the truck stop and pulled slowly into traffic, heading north again. Tina came out from behind the taco restaurant, dumped some coins into the pay phone and dialed the contact number, which would ring once but no voice would answer. She quickly gave her code, location and status, noting especially the rendezvous with the SUV and the second semi. As she hung up and got back on Black Eagle, she wondered what she had just seen.

The two trucks had been parked like two peas in a pod for about ten minutes. Cargo drop-off or pickup? Or maybe an exchange? The nearness of Fort Huachuca and the glimpse of the combat boots made her wonder if some of Uncle Sam's weaponry had been involved. It wouldn't be the first time the drugs for guns swap had been done.

But the SUV driver had only been there for less than five minutes. Tina's guess was that he had been the money part of the equation. Money was small, light, extremely valuable. The way it lent itself to corruption made her view it as obscene.

She rewound her assumptions: Camo Man wasn't necessarily military, despite being smack in the middle of an Army town. He could be a neo-Nazi, part of a drug gang, or even, worst of all, a bent Border Patrol agent. It wasn't out of the question that a rotten apple from some other agency could be in on a shady deal. The temptation of easy money could tempt an agent from the Drug Enforcement Administration or even Alcohol, Tobacco and Firearms, who would be interested in Tina's pursuit if her hunch that weapons were involved proved out.

Arizona also had a headache as state and local law enforcement was increasingly involved because of high-speed chases that led to crashes and bodies scattered along the roadside. An even more disturbing trend was shootouts between rival coyotes as they hijacked loads of drugs or immigrants at gunpoint. They weren't just waving the guns either; blasts of automatic fire from AK-47s had added to the death toll. It was turning into a chaotic war and the governor had threatened to bill the federal government for the state's escalating costs in enforcement and humanitarian care.

Those were just a few of the pieces in a puzzle and Tina hadn't even found an edge piece to put on the table. Vegetable Man's truck rolled ahead of her now, bound for the interstate. And then where: Tucson, Phoenix, Albuquerque, El Paso? And what was its cargo? More miles lay ahead before answers would become clear. She settled into the saddle, knowing that even with full tanks, the semi couldn't outlast Black Eagle's range. Like a lone goose heading north she followed.

\*\*\*\*

# Chapter Four

Tina woke again as the bus lurched to a halt. She peered out the window – halogen lights, another checkpoint near Tubac. A few more tired looking *cruceros* were loaded onto the bus, bottles of water passed out. Tina sipped, a little dizzy, harder to see out of her left eye now. The woman said her daughter in Phoenix was trying to get her into the country. "We used to go up north every summer, follow the fruit harvest, then go back to Mexico in the winter. Now it is so difficult to get in, nobody risks going back and getting stranded."

She dabbed Tina's eye with water. Tina thanked her, then fell back asleep.

But not for long. The bus was rolling to a stop on a ranch road. No lights or checkpoint this time, just a plain white van parked on the shoulder. The bus door opened and a tall guy in a Border Patrol uniform came in, walked up the aisle to the fifth row and stared menacingly at the captives. Tina saw José stand up in the first row, walk down the steps with Señor Blanco trailing close behind, and hand the backpack of cash to the driver of the van. It was the redhead. Standing in front of the van was a scowling Carlos Cabrera, holding an Uzi.

Carlos! That S.O.B. of Mexican mob boss Juan de Ochenta. She had been double crossed.

The rest of the Blanco family quickly filed out the front of the bus and loaded into the van. Tina could see Blanco himself urging Luz into the van and heard her shouting, *"Donde esta Tina?"* The answer came from Carlos as the van's doors closed: "Her work is done."

The guy in the aisle did an about-face and got into the passenger side of the van. As the bus rolled away, the van made a U-turn and headed into the darkness. The whole transfer had taken less than three minutes, leaving weeks of planning to collapse into uncertainty. Tina slumped into darkness.

She dreamed she was dizzy, but when she tried to hold onto her head to keep it from spinning, it came off in her hands, spun around and was shouting at her: *"Quien es?* Who are you? How many names do you have?"

"What's your name? *Su nombre, por favor!"* A guy in uniform asking her.

She took a deep breath, hoping for consciousness to clear. She stretched her plastic-tied hands to her front pocket and pulled out the waterlogged passport Papa had given her at the start of the mission. "Valentina Corazón. Quetzaltenango, Guatemala."

Another deep breath and she fought the dizziness, tried to focus as the guy helped her to her feet. The bus was empty now and the guy helping her didn't seem quite as pushy as the rest of the uniforms had been. At the bottom step another uniform, a woman this time. Tina turned her head against the swirling and managed to step onto the pavement, saw razor wire, a double gate, Wackenhut buses, more lights. The pair herded her into a warehouse lit by buzzing halogen lamps. Steered her over to one corner and put her in a chair at the medic table.

"What happened to her?" Another woman. She checked the numbered tag on Tina's plastic wrist cuffs and typed into a laptop. "The report says she slipped in the tunnel and hit her head on the cement." The desk woman flashed a light in Tina's eyes. "Have her sit over here for observation for awhile."

Tina bobbed in and out of consciousness, heard buses roll in, out, a constant flow of detainees processed then shunted to detention centers or repatriation. As her consciousness cleared, she realized the shotgun blast in Nogales would trigger a report of "shot fired," most likely blowing her cover....or at least putting it to a severe test. Would her mission be accidentally blown by her own former agency?

****

# Chapter Five

That night it had started, blackness ruled the desert north of Fort
Huachuca as Tina piloted Black Eagle. The SUV-truck rendezvous
she had just witnessed put her on hyper-alert. The risk of being
spotted by the truck was even more dangerous now that she knew
there were other potential players in the mix.

She had about a half hour of two-lane country road ahead
before Vegetable Man connected with Interstate 10. She
lagged back, keeping the semi just on the edge of both visual
contact and the range of the radio tag.

Black Eagle rolled smoothly and she took advantage of the
lull to scan the radio traffic, especially any signals from the
truck that might get picked up on her directional antenna. It
was targeted to pick up cellular phone signals, too, but so far
there had been not a peep from the truck. She knew it was
there, though. In addition to the locator blip on her screen, she
had a radar readout that showed him rolling at a conservative
67 m.p.h. She scanned again.

Nothing. The whole rendezvous with the other truck and
the SUV cowboy had been done in radio silence, too. The flip
side of that silence was that if she had been spotted, she might
monitor a message from the truck to whoever else might join
the party.

A scattering of motor home lights on the left marked the
campground at Karchner Cavern. Tina sniffed the night air
and caught a whiff of bat guano from the massive
underground cave. The limestone ridge above the cave
loomed as a jagged black horizon against the scattering of
stars. This trace of the natural world made her a bit nostalgic,
knowing she would have to brace herself for the chaos of
interstate traffic.

As the lights of traffic on I-10 began to glow up ahead, she felt a bit like she was following a salmon upstream to spawn. There could be rapids and shoals, but she was ready.

At the junction, the truck rolled past the fuel plazas and burger joints before turning onto the ramp heading west towards Tucson. Tina rolled to a halt at the most convenient pay phone, called in the code and status update. Less than a minute had ticked off the digital readout on Black Eagle's console by the time she was back on the bike.

Tina knew these roads as well as her ancestors had known the trails and valleys that criss-crossed Navajoland. When she turned sixteen she had talked Papa into getting her a little Honda scooter for her birthday to use when they were in Washington, DC. He had resisted, but her mother reminded him that she had toured the streets of Hanoi on just such a machine when he met her during his tour in Vietnam.

Since Papa split his time between his offices in Washington and Phoenix, it was easier the following year, but not by much, to talk him into getting her a dirt bike for Arizona. Then after Annapolis and her Kuwait stint in the Marines, she had jumped at the chance to get an assignment back home in Arizona working with the Inspector General on thorny issues setting up internal investigations of the Border Patrol.

Tina had earned a reputation for tackling assignments across the map and getting things resolved quickly. Black Eagle had been from the sand dunes of Yuma in the southwest corner of Arizona, up to Window Rock and the Four Corners. From Las Vegas southeastward through Hatch, Las Cruces and Ruidoso, New Mexico, as far as El Paso.

This stretch of I-10 to Tucson started with a long slow climb out of the valley up from Benson, a pocket of rural stagnation that had yet to benefit, or suffer, from the suburban boom that had bloated Tucson and Phoenix. Why move to the desert if you're just going to turn it into Los Angeles without an ocean?

Even at half-throttle she caught Vegetable Man's truck before it made the top of the grade. Rather than play the traffic tango, she rolled off the freeway at each exit, waited for the truck to get ahead, then rejoined the parade. Most of the exits were junctions to nowhere, platted in President Eisenhower's era, at almost regular five-mile intervals, marking rail spurs or ranch roads that had zero traffic.

About 30 miles later the freeway curved northwest around the Rincon Mountains and the glow from Tucson lit the sky in the distance. Tina stayed closer now. Traffic was heavier and she had no trouble ducking behind station wagons, vans and joyriders while keeping the truck in sight. Caution kept her looking in her mirrors, too, in case she spotted anything resembling that SUV from the earlier rendezvous.

There was plenty of radio chatter in her headphones, so she turned the volume down just a bit, listening for anything out of the ordinary. The missing running light on the trailer made the truck easy to spot, so Tina keyed on that as they rolled past the junction with I-19. This dumped traffic coming northward from Mexico into the mix and the road widened to five lanes.

Following the Vegetable Man through Tucson had its own challenges. The perennially crowded stretch of I-10 was swarming with late dregs of rush-hour traffic. The truck rolled along several cars ahead of her. Zigging through the lanes now, Tina spent half her time watching the truck, the other half avoiding street racers weaving through traffic.

The lights of downtown Tucson glowed on the right and to the left, the painted "A" rock pile on "A" Mountain loomed out of the darkness. Tina's senses buzzed at full alert now, smelling food, smokers, diesel fumes, her ears pounded by the stereo thumps of street racers weaving through traffic. Keeping track of the truck kept her focused, as did the intensity of flying through this sea of vehicles on Black Eagle. She had no worries about her abilities to handle the bike, but the watching-out-for-idiots factor kept her fingertips tingling on the handlebars.

After a half hour of suburbia, the perennial construction crunch slowed traffic as it funneled back to two lanes. Ike couldn't have known that building all these freeways would spur a forty-year economic boom that would backfire and clog them with traffic.

Marana in the darkness, a half-moon outlining Picacho Peak ahead on the left. The small farm town a link to her family's past. Victor and Nez had trained here with the Army Signal Corps in the early days of the Code Talkers. It had been the idea of Preston Johnson and when he had started recruiting on the reservation, Victor had been a natural leader to build the first volunteers around. When oil had been discovered in the 1920s, Victor worked with the oil drilling companies to bring as many jobs as possible to native Navajos and make sure some of the proceeds went to fund schools and health facilities on the reservation. Victor's reputation for fairness regardless of traditional clan ties made him respected as *a naat' áanii* or local headman. When the first Navajo Council formed in 1923, Victor became an acknowledged leader among Four Corners men.

Nez had been born in 1926 and attended one of those schools built with the oil money. His English skills were as important to the Code Talker program as the native language. Victor had insisted on taking his young son with him when the military men came and began recruiting of the secret program.

When the first trainees showed up in Marana, Victor was the oldest and Nez was the youngest. Victor had made it clear that he would not be crossing any ocean without taking his son along with him. The code language and alphabet was laboriously drafted from Navajo words.

Nez had shown early aptitude for electronics and radio technology. The math and English skills he had learned at the Navajo school made him a natural fit with the other young trainees from farms and towns around America who were streaming through the desert outpost. Then, before they had shipped off to California for Marine training, Nez had gone on a weekend pass with his father and some other recruits to visit Tucson and the San Xavier del Bac Mission.

Nez had spotted Estrella at one of the food stands that lined the dusty parking lot between the white dome of the mission and the trail that led uphill to a shrine atop a rocky mound. Estrella had only been 13 years old, but when Nez saw her standing under the shade ramada, he had walked up and stood tall but silent in front of her. She, already used to a flood of young Army trainees, chewed him out in Spanish. He had no idea what she was saying, but when she laughed, then handed him a piece of fry bread, he smiled back. The universal language. She spoke a mix of Tohono O'odham and Spanish, which connected poorly with his Navajo and English. Fortunately, they were both fluent in smiles.

Two years later, after the war and now fluent in Spanish he picked up from his shipboard mates, Nez came back to Tucson and began to court Estrella while he attended the University of Arizona on the GI Bill. From then and there the path of Tina's family's history had branched out to include Washington, New York, Vietnam, Kuwait ... the world.

This memory was pushed out by the smell of ostrich guano — a tourist trap at the base of the twin spires of Picacho Peak that sold giant eggs and feed pellets to gullible souls who had never had the chance to get their fingers bitten by an ostrich.

Picacho Peak was itself a misnomer, since *"picacho"* was Spanish for peak. Grandfather Nez had told her stories about how during the war a radio wire stretched between the two spires. The rite of passage was that on their first solo flights the young pilots would steer their AT-6s under the wire.

Traffic volume was still heavy even though it was almost midnight. The trucks came out at night, trying to avoid traffic on the long haul from California to Florida and parts in between. Vegetable Man's semi had been moving with the flow, keeping to a conservative 65 mph. Traffic was still too thick to open it up to 75, the actual speed limit.

A row of derelict motels marked the junction at Eloy that branched east toward the Arizona State Prison at Florence. Tina lagged back, her caution rewarded when she saw the truck exit without signaling. She killed her light, rolled slowly off the shoulder of the interstate and came to a complete stop when she saw that the truck had done the same on the apron of the ramp ahead. She reached behind to the left pannier, flipped open the lid and took a look with the binoculars.

No other vehicles joining the truck. Nothing from the radio scan. Was Vegetable Man going to head for Florence? There was nothing out there but cotton fields, the prison and a scattering of small towns populated by agricultural and prison workers.

The truck started rolling again, easily visible in the flat landscape crisscrossed by farm roads and irrigation canals. Tina followed, headlight off. More than ever, she watched her mirrors and the side roads. The truck began what seemed to be a random series of right and left turns, meandering through the fields.

A few bolls of unpicked cotton shone under the half moon and linty streaks of fluff lined the dirt berms around the fields — the famous Pima cotton renowned for its softness. Cotton warehouses alternated with pecan orchards, forlorn groups of trailers with dirt yards and random palm trees stuck hopefully into the ground decades ago, but now looming in the night like scarecrows with sombreros.

A mile had passed without a turn. West now, back towards Casa Grande she guessed. The freeway split there, Interstate 8 branched west to San Diego, while I-10 continued north to merge into the Phoenix snarl. From Phoenix, it could continue north into Utah, or more likely head for Las Vegas or west to Los Angeles.

Again, she guessed wrong. The truck pulled into one of the huge truck stops at the junction, idled slowly through the vast expanse of parking lots that rimmed the fuel plazas, restaurants and maintenance garages. Tina circled the perimeter, swerving to avoid a couple of miniskirt-clad floozies who obviously wouldn't be driving a semi in those spike heels. Vegetable Man completed half an orbit of the huge parking lot and circled back behind the main cluster of buildings.

Along the back fence, he headed for a sparsely populated stretch of asphalt, targeting a vacant spot in a line of four other rigs.

The shell game again, this time nestled among the four other trucks: two pairs facing east with a narrow space in between. As her quarry squeezed into the gap between the other trucks, Tina boosted her transponder to the level two warning transmission with the ping now at one-minute intervals.

Vegetable Man climbed down from the cab, his face invisible below the brim of a baseball cap. He disappeared between the trailers. Tina watched: Five trucks, jammed together side by side, the lights across the top a glowing band broken only by the missing light on the target semi. The four trailers already in the nest appeared to be plain vanilla white. Tina cut through a gap that connected the truck plaza to a pancake house to her right, keeping the parked quintet in sight as she rolled to a stop. She pulled off her helmet and slipped a black balaclava over her head, assessed the situation and again ducked into a pay phone. This time she ended the coded call with "alphabet soup" letting dispatch know she would be switching to verbal radio contact using a 26-key variable coding — an algorithm she had written herself and figured would be unobtrusive considering the amount of CB and cell phone traffic in the busy junction.

She considered watching from a table inside the pancake house, but there were too many truckers inside and she wanted to avoid any unwanted interaction that could distract her from surveillance. There was no way a woman in tight leather motorcycle gear could sit quietly in this place. She chose to stay in the phone booth, receiver to her ear, pretending to look at the phone book every few minutes.

An hour passed before Tina saw feet suddenly jump down between the trailers. The two outermost trucks slowly peeled off either side and rumbled nose to tail up the on ramp toward Phoenix. Tina wished she could have gotten closer and tagged them with tracking beacons, but it was too risky in the well-lit parking lot. Her focus had to stay with her truck, despite the obvious mission creep.

"Two for you, Phoenix," was all she allowed herself, the voice-activated microphone sending her alert into the radiosphere, casting the two trucks' fate to the reserves she knew lurked in the night. She kick-started Black Eagle and checked the monitor. A couple minutes later the other two semis on either side of Vegetable Man followed suit, rolling nose to tail up the ramp. Again, she sent the alert: "Two more, Phoenix."

Only one truck remained.

What the hell? The lurid mural of vegetables had disappeared from her truck. It was now an unmarked white just like its cohorts. Peel-off camouflage. A shell game if ever there was one. Tina stared at the missing running light to reassure herself that it was the same trailer. Vegetable Man slowly rolled away and took the fork toward Gila Bend and San Diego, now in a plain vanilla package. Tina toggled the coded warning, set the alarm system to level three and rolled out of the parking lot in slow pursuit.

Destination, unknown. Cargo, ditto. Aside from another gas plaza at Gila Bend, there was nothing on the road ahead for 150 miles until Yuma, tucked into the expanse of sand dunes where the Colorado River marked the border with California.

Tina rolled smoothly for a half hour and sorted through a personal brainstorm of possible ideas to explain the semi shell game. None made any sense. What had started out looking like a straight up incoming drug shipment had made enough stops and contacts now to turn the permutations of possibility into a puzzle that gnawed at her. Tina loved puzzles, but this one was all variables with no known clues except two: the illegal border crossing and the tip that had originated inside Mexico sent by her unknown compatriot.

This was a flatter, bleaker desert that rolled past in the darkness. Bleak enough that it had been given to the Tohono O'odham for their reservation. Other chunks, such as the Barry M. Goldwater Air Force Range, were reserved as wide open areas where jets could scream through the air, fire machine guns, rockets and drop bombs. Poor Barry, she thought, he deserved better. When she had been a little girl, she had been certain Goldwater was a photographer. His photos kept showing up in Arizona Highways, and Papa had a signed photo of the Grand Canyon by Barry in the Washington, DC office.

Tonight no jets screamed overhead. Not much traffic, either. It was a long way to Yuma and farther still to San Diego. The infrequent off ramps bore only mile numbers now instead of names, appeared out of the darkness, then vanished when her light rolled by.

Past Gila Bend, the smattering of Central Arizona subdivisions melted away and patchy clouds moved in to cloak the moon. A few gusts of wind. The darkness of a desert night became absolute. Tina stayed as far back from the truck as she could while still keeping it in sight. She switched off her light and the concrete roadway of the interstate became a ribbon of dull silver under the bruised purple of the scattered clouds. They could just as well be on the dark side of the moon now, and she focused on staying within the limit of visual contact.

A good thing, too, as the truck suddenly rolled slower, coasting onto an exit ramp. Tina downshifted through the gears and coasted to the shoulder. The truck turned left under the freeway, crossed and started heading back east on the frontage road. She followed, leaving plenty of cushion, keeping a sharp eye for potholes in the cracked asphalt. It wasn't really a frontage road, she realized. More of an unmaintained access road that curved away from the highway and headed south toward the bombing range. There was nothing out there but tumbleweeds and an occasional abandoned landing strip from Luke Air Force Base and the legacy of training hops in the WWII AT-6s. The truck rolled up to the perimeter fence. Tina grabbed her binoculars in time to see Vegetable Man slide open a should-have-been-locked gate, pull the truck through the fence and push the gate back closed.

This is it. Tina clicked all of her electronic friends to their highest settings and signaled for backup: "Off the grid."

A recon flight should be in the air at this stage, a hot chopper watching from a safe range. She slipped the binocular strap over her shoulder to keep them handy, rode Black Eagle up to the gate and let herself into restricted federal property. A hell of a place to do a drug deal in the middle of the night…or was there more to it than that?

The road through the desert was dirt now, sloping south for miles before a flat dry lake stretched toward the jagged black spine of mountains poking at the starry sky. Lights off, Tina coasted carefully through sandy patches where the road dipped through arroyos. After the first fishtail, she flipped her visor up for better visibility and savored the sweet smell of creosote bushes that always reminded her of desert rain.

No rain tonight; visibility endless but mottled in the cloud shadows, the night colors elusive as water in the desert. Reflected moonbeams made the grey-green spiky vegetation seem to float out to either side of the road. A small plane flew east overhead, following the flight path from San Diego or keeping an eye on her? She watched it long enough to make sure it continued on toward Casa Grande. Ahead, the truck was barely visible, but she couldn't risk getting closer and being spotted at this stage.

The arroyos marked the gradual slope of a ridge that bottomed out ahead where the truck was turning left and heading along the flat perimeter of the dry lake. Tina decided to go overland, traversing the rolling ridges and arroyos.

Black Eagle warmed to the task, tires chewing up the sand and rocks, spitting them out as traction, suspension soaking up the bumps. No grazing was allowed on the gunnery range, but wild critters had left a skein of trails across the rocky ridgelines. The challenge for Tina was to pick the best line, dodge rocks, and watch out for overhanging mesquite and palo verde branches. Rabbits and javelinas were short, so they would scoot along at ground level, not bothered by the branches that could sweep her off her saddle.

All the while keeping the truck in view. It turned directly south now toward a scattering of wrecked buildings, reminiscent of a ghost town, but actually some vintage Quonset huts whose days as hangars were done. A wooden tower with no windows stood silent sentinal for the derelict airfield. Tina pulled behind a mesquite tree, turned Black Eagle's engine off and peered through her binoculars as silence reinforced the lunar desolation.

The truck pulled up to one of the decrepit hangars, the door sliding open as it neared, no squeak, freshly maintained. Vegetable Man was expected. No lights were visible inside the Quonset as the door rolled shut. She fought the urge to sneak closer — the expanse of desert and cracked concrete was simply too open for her to cross.

She remounted her motorcycle without starting it, coasted down the last of the sloping ridge in neutral, and laid it down along the side of an arroyo. A few waist high creosote bushes marked the transition from the sandy wash bottom to the hard-packed dry lake and battered taxiway. Tina crept toward them and whispered into her microphone: "Package delivery."

This final alert would bring her backup chopper into range and she hoped the microphone hadn't picked up the nervous edge in her voice. She crawled down the winding wash, her dark purple leather blending into the moon shadows, and settled in behind one of the bushes. The caliche of the dry lake bed beyond the abandoned buildings glowed a ghostly tan where the scattered moonbeams scraped across it, as if the remnants of the heat waves that rose up during the day had been stored and were now pulsing beneath the surface, rising up into the night like the burrowing creatures who came out into the darkness to feed and frolic.

Minutes crawled by; a few glimmers of moonlight danced along the edges of the slow moving clouds. She couldn't hear anything from the hangar, so Vegetable Man must have turned his engine off. Usually she found silence to be restful, but this silence was as dangerous as a rattlesnake that had stopped shaking its tail. She adjusted the focus of the binoculars, but there was no hint of light around the hangar door. From the corner of her left eye she caught a movement and swung the binoculars around and up to the tower, but saw only shadows between the cracks of the walls. She panned left to right, examining each crack for a silhouette, but couldn't be sure.

An engine cranked over, not a diesel, drawing her focus back to the hangar. From the far end of the hut, another black SUV rolled out and circled slowly to the right along the perimeter of the flatland, painting the darkness with light from a spotlight. Tina flattened to ground, toggled the emergency radio button on the chin strap of her helmet: "Welcoming committee." There was no need for radio silence now.

She was invisible now, but even purple-black leather would show up in that damn spotlight. She rolled slowly back from the creosote bush just as a shot from above ricocheted off a rock near where her helmet had just been. Shit, the sentinal in the tower must have an infrared scope! She ran back up the arroyo, crouching low to keep the shoulder of dirt between herself and the sniper. "Shots fired," she hollered into the mike, no need for code now. "What's your range?" If the chopper was nearby, it would be getting a hot welcome. She listened for a reply but heard only the roar of sudden acceleration from the SUV and a barrage of gunfire from the tower. Another shot splintered a branch on a Palo Verde ahead of her, but the guy was obviously shooting blind now.

Tina pulled Black Eagle up from the sand and kicked the engine to life, triggering the mayday button on her handlebars as she goosed the throttle and climbed up the ridge to get an overview of the scene unfolding below. The SUV had doubled back and was heading uphill about four ridges over. If that was the VIP of the group, they were trying to get away. It would be a rough haul back to the access road, even in an SUV, so Tina decided to head straight into the flat and cut ahead, figuring on the element of surprise and Black Eagle's speed to even her odds against the sniper.

"In pursuit of a black SUV heading for the freeway, do you copy?" she shouted, not sure where her backup was, and spun down into the wash, sand flying as she slalomed around the last of the bushes and shot out into the flat, keeping the hangar between herself and the sniper in the tower. As she hit the runway and blasted into the darkness, a couple other figures ran out of the end of the hangar, AK-47s blazing. She had seen plenty of the Russian automatics in Kuwait: Their rate of fire was great, but accuracy at a distance not good. She was on the edge of their effective range thanks to Black Eagle's acceleration.

"Damn it, where are you guys? The party is scattering!"

About where she estimated the freeway overpass to be, Tina turned up the rocky ridge, hoping she had gotten far enough ahead of the SUV to intercept it.

She was outweighed by the massive truck, but could track it along the escape route until reinforcements arrives. She reached the top of the ridge and saw it all in a flash: The chopper coming to rendezvous from the other side of the freeway, the SUV on the frontage road just about to intersect her off-road scramble, and, worst of all, the semi rolling out of the hangar below and looping back toward freedom.

The helicopter tipped the balance in her favor. As it beamed a spotlight down on the SUV, the truck quickly reversed course and headed back toward the hangar. A chaotic jumble of voices filled the radio scanner, some Spanish, some English. Since she and the chopper weren't talking, it had to be the bad guys. Tina blasted along the access road in pursuit, helped a little by the light from above. As they neared the abandoned base again, she cut downhill hoping to shorten the intercept to the SUV. She slalomed through the bushes and cheat grass, branches clawing at her leathers.

They hit the flat at the same time, the SUV accelerating to her left, but Tina was distracted for a split second by the sight of the semi truck off to her right — it had stopped clear of the hangar and the back doors were opening.

"Abandon pursuit; abandon pursuit!" The warning from the helicopter rang in her ears and as she looked back at the SUV, she spotted a man standing in the sunroof, spraying her with an AK-47. Shooting from a moving car on bumpy terrain compounded the accuracy challenge, and sparks blazed from the rocks around Tina, but she wasn't hit.

She did a power-slide right turn and headed back toward the fringe of bushes and dark arroyos. Her front wheel hit the soft sand and started to bottom out as the next burst of machine gun fire raked the hillside. Missed again, but this time a round exploded on her front rim, flattened the front tire and spun her over the handlebars. The blast of the gunfire and the simultaneous crack of her left collarbone as she hit the ground echoed in her helmet just as it slammed into a rock…hard. Dizzy for a second, she saw the chopper sweep overhead, a blast from its Gatling gun forcing the SUV to detour away from her. She rolled onto her right side and crawled over to Black Eagle, pulled out her gun to return fire and saw double: the helicopter sweeping across the airfield, and the SUV pulling away, back towards the semi truck. Now, another shadow appeared from the cargo hold, carrying a fence post. Then the fence post was on fire, but it was really a guy blasting away at the chopper with a shoulder-fired missile. Boom, fuzzy now, a big explosion….Kuwait, ECM, electronic countermeasures made the missile detonate prematurely. Sparks showered down, Fourth of July fireworks reflected on Black Eagle's gas tank. It's a BMW, not a chopper. The chopper is that thing up in the air shooting at the SUV. More fireworks, flashing lights, sirens, darkness.

\*\*\*\*

# Chapter Six

She saw gray, tried to focus, saw blank walls and cabinets. Hospital. Closed one eye to stop the room from rotating, felt the stab in her left shoulder, gave up to the blackness.

More gray, again the hospital room, but brighter now, and a nurse cranking the bed to help her sit up. Tina sipped something from the cup the nurse held to her lips, yuk, tinny tasting apple juice, then took another nap.

Finally she could move enough to look around, despite the shoulder pain.

The dark suit couldn't disguise the fact that the guy at the door was a guard. Was he custody or protection? Either way you could put him in farmer overalls and he'd still look federal.

Tina tried to call him over, tried to move, watched the room rotate and passed out.

The next time she opened her eyes the guard was still there and so was her father.

He asked her in Navajo: "Can you talk?"

She nodded. He turned to the guard, muttered something she couldn't hear. The guard left.

"I'm glad you're better," he said, still in Navajo. Always their secret way. With Mama it had been French for daily girl talk, but Vietnamese for secrets shared in public.

"What are you doing here, Papa?" She sorted out the many things to be confused about, starting with the explosive end to her mission. Why was he here instead of in his Washington, DC office? And had her mission to track the truck failed?

She was alive, so it couldn't have been a complete dud, but the memory of the explosions in the night didn't bode well. "Who told you I was here?"

He sighed, ran his fingers through the his graying hair, thick on top, short on the sides, still looking like the Marine he used to be. He could be a general, she thought. His sharp eyes looked out from under a strong forehead, the rugged chin below peppered with whiskers a bit thicker than "pure" Navajos because of the part-Mexican heritage of his mother, Estrella.

He stood, went to the window, closed the louvers just a bit more, his tall, trim bearing again harkening to his military tradition. He came back and sat again in the bedside chair, giving her a tender look.

"Don't worry, my daughter. I have much to tell you and more things to ask, but first you should know that your place in this mission was not unknown to me. There are other things outside your mission that we must now share, but I need to know that you are strong enough to go forward."

She looked at him, saw the seriousness, knew that when he would tell the story, it would start at the beginning and weave until it was done.

"Yes, my father, I am strong enough." The formal Navajo style of conversation was their acknowledgement to each other that a serious discussion was about to begin.

A small smile crossed his face, but she sensed that somehow it only started him on the path his story would take, rather than eased his burden.

"You know that when I came back from Viet Nam with your mother and left the Marines, I studied to become a lawyer and eventually joined the government."

She nodded. He had been in the government as long as she could remember. As a girl she would ask "What do you do, Papa?" and he would answer, "Whatever needs to be done."

"You also became a Marine, although it was a surprise to your mother, and since then you have found paths into many other agencies and operations. You now know, too, that the government is big and that no agency is totally what it seems. Many agendas conflict on the surface. Below the surface are more secrets than grains of sands in the desert."

He stood, as if looking far into such a metaphorical desert. Tina had always loved his stories as a little girl. His layers and meanings had challenged her as a child and grown even more intriguing as she grew. Today, however, she sensed that truths she previously had only seen hints of would become clear. He went to the window, lifted a slat in the blinds, looked out at the afternoon.

He sat back down. "You will pardon me, my daughter, if I skip the prologue and merely tell you that I knew of your mission because it was under the peripheral control of my agency. I will tell you more as this situation unfolds, but for now you must understand the situation is, in the traditional jargon, 'need to know' only."

Another fatherly smile, but she saw sadness too, more than just a concern for her injuries. "First let me tell you that some of the men you had tracked were captured, with some unfortunate deaths, of their own causing, falling on the other truck drivers who refused to surrender. Your part in the operation was well and bravely done. That is, in part, one reason why I am here.

"Second, the cargo we captured, or I should say the remains of the cargo, was not drugs as we had originally suspected. Although the explosions destroyed much of it, we were able to identify a substantial part of the contents, mostly weapons, including more of the missiles you saw."

She nodded, listening intently, memories of light and noise fresh in her mind.

"Worse, we found brackets for helicopter mounts…but we don't know where the helicopter is, nor the provenance of the munitions."

He looked down at his hands, breathed deeply, and began again: "The worst news, my daughter, is that our informant who sent the alert has been killed…" The silence of his pause brought a cold chill to her heart. She held out her hand and he took it. "I'm sorry, but it is my job to tell you. It was Ruben."

No helmet could have prevented the explosion of memory and pain that hit her head. Ruben, cousin Ruben, protector and inspiration. Ruben pretending to chew her out on the parade ground at Annapolis. Ruben flying a helicopter on the deck to evac her from Kuwait City.

How the hell had she not known he worked for the same agency? Even though it had been years since she had seen him, an occasional cryptic note showed up at their family home in Scottsdale: a postcard covered with mixed metaphors, trick phrases, anagrams and multilingual *chistes*.

She closed her eyes as the tears welled up. The painful ripping of her memories was eclipsed only by the thought of a future with only blackness where Ruben should have been.

She listened to her father's silence, her own breath, the muffled hospital sounds from the corridor. The minutes stretched. The tears finally ebbed. The past, the now, the future still existed. She opened her eyes and began what she knew would be another trail that she could not avoid.

"How was he killed?"

"It was quick, gunshots without warning, after the truck you followed was captured. He was still in Nogales and would have had no reason to see it coming. There was no way he could have known the extent of what we saw happening here in Arizona.

"The other trucks were also captured, but only the drugs were found on them. We are slowly piecing together our long view of what is taking place."

She imagined chaos scattered across the landscape. More episodes in the daily barrage of chaos that those who knew the truth were beginning to call the Border War.

"How can I help?"

"That is exactly why I am here. My challenge has now become even greater. I need someone I trust."

He stood, went to the window and opened the louvers once more to the pink and gold of night's approach. "Your mother is flying in from DC late tonight. I will pick you up tomorrow at 0800," he pronounced it in the military style "eight hundred hours." "I will take you to the house and tell you more as you grow stronger."

"I will do what needs to be done, my father."

The familiar phrase brought a smile to his face. He turned from the window and came to her bedside. She patted him on the shoulder as he gave her a gentle hug, avoiding any pressure on the broken collarbone. She knew not to ask questions, not just because of "need to know" security, but also because starting with fairy tales and legends during her childhood he always told her his stories in the Navajo way, building the castle one brick at a time. In this story she sensed there would be many dragons.

As he turned to leave, she asked him to tell the guard to post outside the door. Now that she was awake she wanted to do some thinking in private.

The door closed behind him and silence filled the room. More memories and sadness were sure to come, but now Tina needed to take inventory. Holding the bed rail, she stepped over the side and was relieved to be able to stand without too much dizziness. Two steps got her to the sink and a cold, wet washcloth to wipe her eyes awake with one hand.

She looked at the bruising on the left side of her forehead, punctuated by a small bandage and a light gauze wrapped around her head. Thank goodness for the helmet. The stiffness in her neck told her she was lucky not to be a quadriplegic after the impact with the rock.

She took a deep breath, met the resistance of the butterfly brace that pulled her shoulders back to keep her collarbone in place, accentuating her cleavage under the periwinkle hospital gown. A separate sling kept her left arm immobile, the hand near her sternum, making her look like a mummified Napoleon.

Well, a tall Napoleon, and the French genes showed most clearly in her eyebrows. Full and slightly arched, they accentuated the strong cheekbones and high forehead of the native mix of Navajo and Tohono O'odham. Her nose was not quite as fine as Mama Michelle's, aside from having been broken in a boxing match at Annapolis, but the Vietnamese/French influence was there and also seen in her complexion. Her skin was a tawny cream, leading some to guess she was Italian, or Brazilian, or Greek, or….

Many times she and Mama had played tricks at embassy parties. Mama would introduce her to the Italian ambassador, for example, and Tina would launch into an enchanting Holly Golightly monologue in perfect Italian. Then Mama would bring over the Greek ambassador, "Pardon the interruption but please meet …" and then the Italian's jaw would drop as the scenario was repeated in Greek.

Soon a group of six or eight fawning men would have been drawn in and finally some one would demand "Who is she, really?" And Mama would say, "Gentlemen, may I introduce my daughter Valentina Nguyen-Desjardins-Toledo." Heady stuff for a 15-year-old.

The blend of ethnicities had let her camouflage her identity across a variety of geographies:  Mexico, Colombia and Guatemala on temporary assignment with the DEA, and — with the Burkha — Kuwait, Saudi Arabia, Syria and Lebanon during the Gulf War and the new century's chaos.

Another cool washcloth and she retreated to the bed. The night sounds of the hospital were tranquil, but her memories had too many explosions, too many bodies.

She turned to her favorite coping meditation in an effort to lull herself to sleep. The fatigue helped. She was barely able to recite the first hundred digits of pi before falling asleep just past the double fours…

****

# Chapter Seven

Dawn. A loose blouse, jeans and sandals sat on the bedside chair when Tina opened her eyes. She pushed the buzzer and let the nurse help her dress. Breakfast didn't appeal, but she forced down a couple bites of egg and some of the syrupy peaches.

When the nurse took out the tray, the guard rolled a wheelchair into the room. Tina knew the rules, so she climbed in for the ride to the door. When they got to the lobby, he left her at the door, went out and scanned the sidewalk. Papa rolled up a minute later in his old blue GMC station wagon and Tina stepped into the sun.

They rolled without speaking through the tasteful winding avenues, lawns of manicured, multicolor gravel, and houses of Santa Fe style stucco arches accented by clumps of desert plants that passed for landscaping in Phoenix. The rolling swale of a golf course was punctuated by a faux lake centered around a fountain of reclaimed wastewater that irrigated the greenery. Scottsdale reminded Tina of a giant putt-putt golf course compared to the sweeping mesas and sheer cliffs of the Navajo reservation. Worst were the shopping malls, which had grown into Disney-ish parodies of bloated consumerism.

Still, people had to live someplace. Tina was the first in her family to be born "off reservation," but Saigon was a distant memory, Washington, DC, held many flashbacks of growing up, and she was far from the roots that drew her back to Navajoland. After Annapolis, her life had been a series of TDY — temporary duty assignments around the world.

She looked over at Papa: He steered the old blue truck through the suburban maze, staying to the right lane as a steady stream of BMWs, Mercedeses and Priuses passed them…or would it be Prii or Prioria she wondered. Not as big an automotive conundrum as why Chevrolet had ever thought to name a car Nova, or *"no va"* in Spanish, meaning "doesn't go."

Scottsdale thinned out as they approached the edge of the Salt River Indian Reservation. Right now, right here with her father, this was home. Her meandering travels around the world brought her back, always, to the roots of family. The Middle Way of Mama's Buddhism wasn't a straight line. Here in the Arizona sun, it turned right onto a dirt road that disappeared into the desert.

Tina could see "Eagle's Nest" ahead on the ridge, blending into the rocky escarpment. A stranger driving the same road could miss it. Grandfather Nez had built the house in the 1950s using native stone and it hugged the base of Thompson Peak. As they climbed the gravel drive, Tina saw Taliesin West in the distance. A monument to Frank Lloyd Wright's creativity, it had always impressed Tina more as a colorful sculpture than as a functional home: the Isadora Duncan of architectural masterpieces, it flaunted color and form much like a dancer skilled with silken scarves.

Papa wheeled into the turnaround at the end of the drive and parked under a Palo Verde tree. Tina opened the door and climbed out. Looking back toward Phoenix, she remembered nights thirty years ago when she would sit out with Mama Michelle, Grandfather Nez and Grandmother Estrella looking at the distant lights. Year by year, the lights crept closer and tendrils of the city reached far into the desert. Now it was the desert that remained as tendrils, rugged washes curving across the landscape, unable to be tamed during the flash flood season.

The smell of fresh-baked croissants filled the kitchen.

Mama was in her bedroom "just cleaning up." Her dark hair was in a bun and she wore a peach colored *ao dai*. She gave Tina a careful hug, then held her at arm's length, giving the bruising along her left temple a detailed examination. The bandage had been removed this morning, revealing a thin line of sutures slightly below the hairline.

"Oh, honey," she said in Vietnamese, "don't you think it's time you settled down with a nice man and stayed at home to work on your *Pho Ga* and *Bánh bao?*"

"Sure, Mama, just like you settled down with Papa so you could go to a different Washington party every night and whisper in the corners."

They both smiled, nudge-nudge-wink-wink, about the clandestine chats and exotic social life her mother led as a "cultural attaché" in parallel to her father's more subdued bureaucratic routine. At least it had always looked subdued on the surface. Now Tina wasn't so sure.

Mama helped her load some clothes into her backpack. Then they went downstairs to join Papa for the croissants and coffee.

"I wish I could go up to Teas Toh with you," Mama said. "But I have to go to New York tomorrow to help present a report to the U.N. from the land mine commission."

Tina was proud of her mother's work to rid Vietnam and Cambodia of the mines left from years of war. She had accompanied her mother a few years back on a mission to bring artificial limbs to mine victims. The visit was rewarding, but the country Tina saw was not the Vietnam of her memory. As with the urban-crazed Chinese to the north, the leaders of the land of her birth were focused on high-profile development, leaving behind the housing and education needs of the people at street level.

"Rats," Papa said. "I read they're training rats to sniff out the mines now. Cheaper than dogs and lighter — don't trigger the mines."

Tina took a sip of Mama's coffee, French roast, of course, rich with sweetened condensed milk. "What keeps the rats from running away?"

"Leashes," he said. "Little strings around their necks. Plus they get a food pellet when they find a mine. The handlers work them in teams."

Mama put another croissant on Tina's plate. "It's good that the mines are being cleared, but it has taken too many years and too many lost legs or deaths. Still, we do what must be done."

Tina exchanged a glance with her father.

In Vietnamese, her mother said, "Don't tie knots and then lose your scissors."

"I understood that," Papa said. "Something about shoelaces."

They all laughed. Tina was happy to share these moments. They seemed rarer in the past few years.

Mama forbade Tina from cleaning up, then said, "I have to duck up to the store for a couple items. Is there anything you two want to pack and take with you to Nez and Estrella's?"

"A new pair of scissors?" Tina said. Mama gave her a gentle hug, then slipped through the door to the garage.

They watched Michelle driving away in her light blue Miata, the knobby truck tires a utilitarian touch for the rugged roads. A stillness filled the kitchen. Tina topped off their coffee cups and followed her father down the hall to his office. He punched in a seven digit code, waited, then added five more. A muted click and he pushed the door open.

Inside, the office looked over the Superstition Mountains to the left and the proverbial "Valley of the Sun" to the right. Phoenix was shrouded by smog. Tina looked at the familiar photos on the wall: Chester with the Udall brothers Morris and Stewart, Grandfather Nez Toledo at a reunion of the Navajo Code Talkers, Tina and her parents at her Annapolis graduation.

The oldest photo was a small black-and-white print of Great-Grandfather Victor and the young boy Nez standing in front of an oil rig. The writing was too faint to read, but the Model A Ford in the background dated it to the early 1930s. A later shot showed them in uniform, Diamond Head in the background. Family history from WWII through Vietnam up to the present: Chester with Presidents Carter, Reagan and Clinton. A photo of him and Michelle on a return to Vietnam toward the end of the century. Snapshots of places and time that marked a family on the edges, and sometimes in the center, of history.

The desk was functional and solid rather than flashy. Tina sat down and put her coffee cup on a polished disc of petrified wood. Her earliest memory of the office was as a girl, being shooed out by Grandfather Nez whenever the old black telephone would ring. Then Papa had come back from Vietnam and eventually joined the law firm. The whole family had spent more time here, but then Nez retired and he and Estrella moved back to Teas Toh on the reservation.

Tina had shared many chats with her father in this office over the years. He had tried to talk her out of going to Annapolis, unsuccessfully, but had supported her continuing career choices. In many ways, her path mirrored his. After his tours as a Marine, he had gone to law school, as his father before him, and become heavily involved in issues dear to the hearts of Arizona, namely water and other environmental causes. Tina had been 12 years old when they had first moved to Washington, DC Visits to Phoenix were fewer, the bulk of the law firm's work done by associates while Papa kept busy, Tina had thought, lobbying a spectrum of agencies, well placed officials and business interests.

As the years had passed, the issues had changed. More recently it had been "immigration and border security." In other words, keep the Mexicans out. Nobody was talking about putting a fence across the bottom of Canada.

The main detour Tina had taken was to steer away from the legal profession. She had become hooked on science: specifically electronics, computing and telecom. Putting together the right proprietary chip designs and algorithms had made her much in demand for "secret sauce" in a variety of assignments, usually funded by Uncle Sam, always highly classified.

Chester took a key from his pocket, opened a desk drawer and took out a manila envelope. "This is official," he said, in English, handing her the envelope. "You're on an extended medical leave, with orders to report to headquarters when you're fit for duty again. You can pass the word about a transfer among your friends and co-workers, say you're going to spend some time at Diné Bikéyah with Grandfather Nez but for all intents and purposes it will stand as a goodbye."

Diné Bikéyah, Navajoland, thousands of square miles of open space that would be able to hide dozens of her, hundreds of her. Deep cover, wide open cover, gone away "poof" disappeared cover. Tina knew nothing yet of the organizational structure or operation she was getting into, but it was obvious to her that she was being cut loose from her past ties and was about to vanish without a trace.

Not that her ties were that strong. It always seemed that projects, places and people rotated through her life. An apartment, furnished, in Tucson was about it for this latest undercover job with the Inspector General sorting through the Border Patrol leaks. Four months so far. About enough time to connect with a few distant Tohono O'odham and Mexican cousins in the area.

What was she doing? Who did she work for? Whenever they asked, she trotted out some mumbo jumbo about General Services Administration and computer file management revisions. That always worked to steer the conversation in a more interesting direction, such as the Wildcat basketball team and could the U of A go to the Final Four this year.

No Tucson boy friend.

None in Albuquerque or Livermore during the assignment last year either. She had spent too much time bouncing back and forth trying to seal a leak in the Sandia National Laboratories. The fact that she found out too late that she was the bait instead of the trapper still pissed her off.

Maybe after this next assignment she should park someplace for awhile, select a path worth sticking to.

She opened the envelope and looked at the cover sheet: No heading or letterhead, just a plain sheet of paper with a short note over her father's signature releasing her from prior duties for a "special assignment."

Subsequent pages, all on letterhead, detailed discharges and service dates from an alphabet soup of federal agencies: The U.S Marine Corps, Department of State (a short assignment), NASA (some electronics work), Treasury, CIA (redacted, of course), and finally the Inspector General, personally signed, her recent "Border Patrol" assignment.

The cover letter, medical status report and transfer documents were detailed and extensive, yet vague enough to give no clue of what was to happen next. Even less clear to her was how her own father got to be involved. She had always known he was in "the government," but over the years she had never really tried to pin down what he did. She had always assumed he was a specialist in legal issues and involved with a succession of Inspectors General, interstate commerce nabobs or higher-ups at Defense or State, sometimes even the periphery of the White House. It had appeared to her that he had the ears of several heads of departments, but not that he was a head himself. Today he was wearing the hat.

She put the papers back in the envelope and gave him a tight smile. "Very tidy package, Papa, but who's pulling the strings on this?"

"Honey, if I knew, I'd have to be a good soldier and lie to you." His tone was casual now, poker game rapport as cards were turned over and real hands were compared to the façade that had been bluffed. "You've spent enough time along the border to know that the crap is getting deep on both sides. We're going to give you the best shovel we can, but you're getting sent out to do some deep digging. Solo."

He gave her a small look of concern, mixed with pride. "If I didn't think you could pull it off, I would have told them to send someone else's daughter. It's not too late to back out."

She set the envelope on the edge of his desk, took a sip of her coffee. "You knew I wouldn't back out right from the start. If you thought I would hesitate, you wouldn't have even brought me this far."

She saw his jaw loosen, a smile not quite moving into his brown cheeks, his eyes listening.

"So why a woman, why me?"

"For the same reason you put on a burqa to get into Kuwait before Desert Storm. Some men will give you a look for the wrong reasons, but for most of them you will be invisible. As for why you, I told you last night I needed someone I can trust." He switched to Navajo: "There have been leaks inside this organization that could wreck not only the operation, but leave our entire mission more vulnerable. I need you to find not only a killer, but who he works for."

Ruben was dead. Tina had faced danger before, but now she wondered if the personal urge for revenge she felt would tip her balance, cloud her thinking. No. Ruben would tell her to fly straight, aim well, wait to shoot.

Papa reached into the drawer again and pulled out a battered leather folder embossed with the maze of I'itoi. The burnished brown of the leather had a warm shine, while the black maze circled around to beckon the figure of the man at the entry into the winding trail that would be his life. She had seen the folder before: Grandfather Nez had made it and given it to Papa when he graduated from Annapolis in 1966. When she had been a girl, the folder was often on his desktop when she ran through his office. He would let her run her fingertip over the maze, tracing the convoluted path to the center, but if she tried to pick it up he would shoo her away with a warning about "important papers." Now he was handing the folder to her.

She ran her hands over the smooth surface, looked at him.

"Go ahead, open it," he said, switching to his conversational English. "This is the background as it stands. I have to go back to DC for a week to pull some strings. I'm going to take you up to Teas Toh in the morning tomorrow so you can stay with Nez and Estrella. Heal, read through the file, think about my warning. You'll be getting dropped into the middle of the rattlesnake's nest surrounded by bad guys…you might have to practice up on lying. I don't know if that's a language you speak."

He pointed at the manila folder she had taken out of the leather case. "I haven't gotten to say this for awhile, but after you read these, you should burn them. When you see what we're up against, a sacred fire might be a wise choice."

She heard Michelle's Miata rolling up the driveway. Chester walked over to the wall and swung a painting of the Grand Canyon aside, revealing a safe. "Let's put them in here and you can get them after lunch."

When they went down to the kitchen, instead of *Pho Ga* and *Bánh bao,* it was cheese enchiladas, chile verde tacos and guacamole, one of Papa's family traditions. He gave Michelle a hug and took an appreciative sniff of the platters arranged on the table.

"I called Nez and Estrella to let them know we were coming," he said, grabbing Mama's hand. "Grandmother said she would make some fresh tamales, so if Valentina and I don't eat them all, I'll bring some back for you."

Tina smiled and saw Mama doing the same at Papa's teasing use of her "girl" name. When she had become a sophisticated teenager in Washington, D.C, she had decreed that henceforth she would be known by the more adult sounding "Tina."

Names had come and gone since then. As a plebe at Annapolis the most common monikers had been "swabbie" or worse.

The conversation over tacos was primarily about how Nez and Estrella were holding up pretty well as their odometers rolled into the 80s. Tina relaxed as the familiar view of Camelback Mountain in the distance combined with the homey kitchen smells to give her a sense of safety. More dragons lay ahead, but not now, not here.

Upstairs in her room she looked at the manila folder: The string clasp was held in place by a lump of wax stamped with the maze of I'itoi. She broke the seal and studied the dossier — the French term always seemed so secretive, hinting at much to know. For starters, the first terse sheet said that she had been placed on medical leave and that subsequently, when it was determined she had sufficiently recuperated and was fit for reassignment, she would be transferred to "liaison duty."

In other words, she was going to disappear.

There was more, plenty of it. An extensive analysis detailed how the American war on drugs had combined with the "border security" enforcement to actually destabilize the situation. The increased enforcement drove up costs for illegal border crossers, giving a billion dollar windfall annually to the coyotes who trafficked in people and drug mules.

Mexico's efforts to battle the problem had taken a horrible turn: The Mexican government had formed an elite commando group called Grupo Zeta to battle the drug lords. The U.S. had helped, training the elite "special forces" of the Mexican military at the School of the Americas at Fort Benning, Georgia.

When the Zetas returned to Mexico, the drug lords proved that money trumped patriotism by simply hiring them away from the Mexican government.

As Tina sat on her bed and turned the pages of the sordid history of bloodshed, bribery and intimidation, she couldn't help but think of Star Wars and the lure of turning the "Force" to the Dark Side. She remembered being a little girl who wanted to fly in space like Luke Skywalker, but had settled for Marine helicopters instead.

She thought about the helicopter mounts found in the truck wreckage and understood the growing concern over the increasing violence in Mexico. Grupo Zeta quickly grew increasingly powerful, openly flaunting the often out-gunned *federales* south of the border. As the drug war between the Gulf Cartel to the east and the Tijuana Cartel to the west began to heat up, it grew far beyond mere assassinations of rival leaders.

The Zetas began carrying out extensive killings of government officials, law enforcement officers and even journalists or singers who had spoken against the growing lawlessness. The report noted the Zetas were regarded by U.S. law enforcement officials as expert assassins, especially worrisome because of their elite military training, penchant for using AR-15 and AK-47 assault rifles, and the growing ruthlessness of their methods, including beheadings and posting of execution videos on the internet.

Who killed Ruben? Beyond that, how had they broken Ruben's cover? And could being a woman help her get inside and find answers to those questions?

She took a break between sections of the document and opened her curtains to let in the late afternoon light. The sun was about two fingers over the horizon. Her parents had left for a dinner with friends and she enjoyed having the quiet house to herself. Papa had added this wing of the house himself, stone by stone, after they came from Vietnam. He had studied law at Arizona State after he left the Marines, and Mama had found a job helping resettle the flood of Vietnamese refugees. She and Tina had both learned Spanish quickly during their six-month stay with Nez and Estrella, so Michelle's trilingual English-Spanish-Vietnamese translation skills had been in big demand. There hadn't been much need for French, so she and Tina had kept it as their choice for daily gossip.

Tina laid her unbruised cheek against the cool stone framing the window and pondered the quiet that surrounded her compared to the anticipated chaos and uncertainty of the mission ahead. There had always been interludes of tranquility in their lives. Even as her father's law practice had grown and he had been increasingly involved in Washington politics, he had insisted on spending the winters in Arizona. Said he needed it for his personal *Hozho*, the balance of life so important in the Navajo tradition. "Or it could be *Himdag*," he used to kid her. "Go ask Grandmother Estrella."

*Hozho*, the Navajo concept of harmony and balance that pervaded, and guided, a life well lived. Tina felt that riding Black Eagle came close to perfect harmony if *Hozho* could have wheels.

*Himdag*, the similar concept in the Tohono O'odham tradition, encompassed virtually every facet of life. Tina had come to realize that this "way to be" was more than some abstract concept, and that it permeated the traditions in not only the Navajo and Tohono O'odham ways, but in similar forms throughout the Native American tradition.

The irony to her was that she had grown up steeped in the Middle Way of Mama's Buddhism, as well as the straight path of Jesus taught to her as a girl by the nuns in Saigon. The sum of all the teachings had such a harmony to them that they blended into one in her mind. Now she would have to decide which one gave the best sanction to revenge. She comforted herself with the goal that finding Ruben's killer would restore balance somehow. It wouldn't bring him back, but if he were in her position, he would give it everything — whatever needed to be done.

But that could wait for tomorrow. As the sun blipped out, a small relapse of dizziness reminded her that she was on injury leave. And Mama had put fresh sheets on her bed. On her way there she took one last glance in the mirror. The bruising was changing colors from the previous purple-blue to a more flesh-toned brownish-green. Yuk. She noticed that the suture line pulled her left eyebrow up a tiny bit, an inadvertent mini-facelift that softened the crow's feet at the corner of her eye and gave her a slightly curious look.

****

# Chapter Eight

Mama made French toast and a thermos of coffee the next morning before kissing them both goodbye. She rolled off down the hill in the Miata to catch her flight to New York.

Papa had his "Navajo" outfit on: faded jeans, plaid shirt, scuffed Red Wing boots. Tina had chosen a loose blue blouse that was easy to get on over the shoulder brace. The butterfly contraption was still in place, but she had stopped using the sling.

When they went into the garage, Tina noticed a familiar shape in the corner. The tarp covered Black Eagle, but she could see the mangled front wheel. Her leathers, marked with a few scrapes but otherwise undamaged, hung on a peg behind the bike.

She crossed over, lifted the tarp and examined the bullet holes in the tank and fairing. Her bike was wounded and so was she. She dropped the tarp and went to get into Papa's truck, but saw Ruben's face in her memory.

Papa backed the truck out of the garage, punched in the alarm code on the keypad and watched the door slide shut. They rolled down the driveway wrapped in their individual thoughts.

North out of Scottsdale, Chester skipped I-17 and drove state highway 87 up through the rolling desert that would eventually give way to scattered juniper and pine scrub as they rolled north and gained altitude.

Papa was first to break the silence: "This is a volunteer ops, so don't be afraid to bail out at any time."

"How could I? You never bailed. You flew down on the deck to bring Mama and the Nuns and babies out of Hanoi, then kept going back to the embassy roof until the Viet Cong got to the fence.

"Before that, Grandpa and Great-Grandpa went out into the ocean to be Code Talkers. That had to be like going to another planet after a life in the desert."

Outside the window, that desert was giving way to canyons and cottonwoods that lined the winding road as it followed the streambeds cut into the Mazatzal Mountains.

"I'm already in this," Tina continued, pointing to her bruised head. "I owe it to Ruben. It's a family tradition: We do what needs to be done."

Her father nodded, looked back to the highway. "I was afraid you'd say that, but not surprised. If I had any major concerns, I wouldn't have tapped you for the mission."

The road dipped and climbed over the next several miles as it gradually gained altitude toward Payson and the Mogollon Rim looming in the distance.

They slowed as they hit the outskirts of Payson and rolled through dusty pine trees that edged the roadway. The town traffic was scattered — not many people driving between the rows of used cars, vintage strip malls and dusty supermarket parking lots that were a staple of small town Arizona.

Then Papa shifted into a lower gear for the more serious climb up the Mogollon Rim. Partway up the nearly 2,000-foot gain in altitude, Tina's ears popped.

Papa pulled over at a turnout and hauled out one of his water cans to aid a motorist whose steaming car had tired of climbing the grade with the air conditioner on.

Tina stepped out of the truck and savored the smell of pine and the glorious sunshine that painted the cliffs with light and shadow. Many times she had flown over this huge slab that marked the southern edge of the Colorado Plateau.

Nature had left its claw marks along the serrated cliffs, softened in places by dots of junipers and scrubby pines. The hardy trees marked where the rain clouds scraped over the edges and the upward pressure of the rim squeezed the water out of them like a sponge. Unfortunately, it was usually a fairly dry sponge.

Samaritan stop completed, Papa drove to the top of the rim and took a break at the summit overlook.

Behind them to the south the clear day made the layers of ridgelines they had traversed look like waves of green rolling upward to crash on the rocky shore of the Mogollon.

Ahead, the top of the plateau flattened out into a wonderland of buttes, striped in golds, grays and reds by layers of sandstone capped with the harder igneous rock that gave them their tabletop shapes.

They munched on sandwiches and savored Michelle's coffee from the thermos. An occasional car rolled by. The tranquility made it hard for Tina to believe this was a world of bullets, rockets and explosions. She took comfort in knowing that this moment gave balance to the chaos past and future.

They crossed the Burlington Northern Santa Fe tracks and Interstate 40 at Winslow, the big road stretching east into the distance toward Holbrook, Gallup and Albuquerque. Chester bypassed the interstate entirely, rolling slowly along the ghost of Route 66 through town to get to the continuation of highway 87 north.

Tina hummed the old Eagles tune "Take it Easy" as they passed "Standin' on the Corner Park" the city had created to capitalize on the tourism: The bronze statue of the hitch hiker with his guitar was backed by a mural of "a girl, my Lord, in a flatbed Ford…"

More historically significant, she thought, was the Lorenzo Hubbell Trading Post, one of the dozens of outposts the Hubbell family had scattered around the landscape beginning in the 1870s. Lorenzo was the Sam Walton of his day, Tina mused, but now the remaining posts were historical sites.

They rode quietly out of town, but Tina knew her father was also remembering the family history that was scattered throughout this area much like the mini-mesas that dotted the landscape in the Hopi Buttes area: small escarpments that looked from the air like droplets of paint that had fallen off God's brush when he had made the big swaths of the Hopi mesa and Monument Valley.

"I have a question, Papa."

"Just one?"

"Touché. How about for starters, who do you work for?"

He thought about that for awhile, slowing the truck as a camper up ahead lumbered into a left turn toward Homolovi State Park. The scattered remains of some Anasazi ruins marked the edge of Navajoland.

In the time of history, the rubble marked the transition between the disappearance of the pre-Columbian Anasazi and the emergence of the Hopi. For Tina, the threads of time and place that wove their way through this ancient desert were a reminder of the smallness of her own existence in the skein of the universe.

In their driving, the park marked one more hour of increasingly remote roads to the hogan of Grandfather Nez and Grandmother Estrella.

"The home stretch," he said, turning off the paved road that continued on to Second Mesa. He slowed the truck to a comfortable relationship with the washboard and bumps of the first of many miles of dirt. "Who I work for, or should I say 'we' work for now, goes back to post-WWII. You know that your great-grandfather was one of the first Code Talkers and that Nez went with him to the Pacific."

Tina nodded, sensing that she knew only what she had seen on the surface.

"After the war, Nez went back to the U of A while Victor went to Washington, DC, with Chester Nimitz, my namesake. Nez can fill you in on the details, but the post-war era was pretty chaotic for the winners as well as the losers."

He put on the brakes to avoid a roadrunner darting across the road. The grey-black bundle of feathers disappeared into the brush. "By the time Nez graduated and got his law degree, the OSS had started to morph into the CIA. Not everybody was happy about some of the dirty tricks going on in secret. Even Eisenhower warned about the 'military industrial complex.'"

The terrain began to climb, the scrubby vegetation shrank lower by the mile, as if sinking below the earth as the dirt rose. He turned right onto a smaller road with no trace of gravel. "A small organization we'll call 'the good guys' operated behind the scenes on an informal basis. When John Kennedy became president he kicked it into high gear and it started to expand exponentially, but I can tell you officially that we still operate unofficially."

"*Yei'bi'chi*," Tina said, thinking of the invisible spirits represented by the *kachinas*.

"More invisible than the 'spooks' reputation of the CIA. There was a big Arizona connection in the 1960s: Kennedy appointed Stewart Udall as Secretary of Interior and his brother Mo took over his seat in the house. The southwest had nuclear testing, missile silos and U-2 training flights."

"And the good guys."

He nodded, but gave her a serious look. "Unfortunately, after forty years and many operations worldwide, we're not so secret any more, at least to the bad guys. I'm afraid I have more bad news about Ruben."

The road reached a fork and Chester took the left branch. Just past the intersection, the dirt track hugged the base of a cliff. He pulled the truck to a stop in a slim wedge of shade and signaled for a break.

A shelf on the bottom edge of the cliff made a cool seat. Tina carried a bottle of water with her, sat by her father and offered it to him.

He declined, took a deep breath, and pushed forward with his news: "Rubens' body was dumped in the center of the Maze of I'itoi at the Morris Udall Community Center in Tucson the day after we intercepted the trucks."

Tina closed her eyes, squeezed back yet another wave of tears. The symbolism slowly dawned on her. The Udalls, Mo and Stu, were longtime family friends and the plaza with the circular maze was symbolic of the brothers' efforts over the years on behalf of the Tohono O'odham and other Indians in Arizona.

"You're on the tail edge of one operation that has had mixed results," her father continued. "I will leave you with another folder that has more extensive details of the current situation, but the next stage of your involvement won't be defined until I get back next week. You should be able to count on at least five days of rest while I huddle in DC. If there are updates, I'll send them to you on the SATCOM link."

Tina smiled at the incongruity: Here in the middle of the Four Corners, her family's history of undercover work for the government was symbolized by a shiny disc pointed at the sky.

"There's still a lot we don't know. You have to be used to that in this business. It stinks, but that's the way it is. In any other case, you would have been left in the dark. But this is different, I started the goddamn trace because I thought I saw …"

He paused, took a breath, looked away. Tina realized her father was now a *Viejo*, an old man, spare with his energy, especially now that he seemed to be weighing ancient burdens.

He shook his head, inhaled, turned back to look her straight in the eye. This was the cold-blooded spymaster now, not the patient Navajo: "It was my call to put *orejas* in Mexico. It's been building for three years. The signal you followed was our biggest lead in the past year. Ruben got close to the center, close enough so that when we made the intercept, he was trapped inside. If I had known the full situation, I would have pulled him out." He looked down at his hands, squeezed the gnarled knuckles together.

Tina knew he was thinking of the bloody body dumped at the center of the maze in Tucson. There was something personal about it. The center was named in honor of Morris Udall and her family's links to the Kennedys and the roots of the GG were slowly becoming clear to her. The way Ruben's body was placed in the center of I'itoi's maze at the feet of the Basket Woman statue was also a clue that the perpetrators knew who they were dealing with.

"On the surface it's another case of trading drugs for guns," her father continued. "The quantities are bigger, but it could pass for a volume deal by regular trading partners. Unfortunately, it's actually the point of contact of a system that's much bigger and more sinister. Starting from the Mideast, through Europe and into South America, we've been trying to choke off the biggest network of arms dealers in the world. It's only one step below the threat posed by Korea and Iran in their search for nuclear materials."

He let the hint of a smile cross his face. "We're leaving them to our cousins in the CIA."

Tina offered the water again. This time he took a sip. "Our problem is that we're dealing in a huge international flow of weapons, cash and drugs that parallels the legal trade. Stuff is always 'falling off the truck' and the money is so huge that military and government officials take the bait, even here in the U.S. Maybe I should amend that to say especially here in the U.S. since our military-industrial complex, as Ike called it, is the biggest in the world. The competition is Russia and China."

A turkey vulture floated by, saw that they weren't food and continued on, circling back to catch an updraft from the heat above the cliff.

Tina remembered the traces left behind in the wreckage of the truck she had followed.

"You mentioned the helicopter mounting brackets we found. What's that tell us?"

"Unfortunately, they were for an Apache, but that's mostly troubling because it pins the source down to the U.S. They were new, which means a supply sheet someplace got altered or a database entry was erased. Computers are labor saving devices for the bad guys, too."

He stood, stretched. Tina did the same and walked with him back towards the truck. She thought about the transfer she had witnessed during the first stop Vegetable Man made in Sierra Vista, remembering the boots and camouflage pants she had seen under the trailer. Maybe Camo Man had been military after all.

"Where's the helicopter?"

"That's question number one," he said. "Question number two is, are there more than one? The obvious question number three is who's building their own private air force? Answering those questions should also lead to the bastard who murdered Ruben."

He started the engine and shifted into low gear. The big station wagon lumbered over the bumps on the last stretch toward a trio of small mesas ahead, the hogan just a dot four miles in the distance.

"The situation between the drug gangs, the Mexican government and the paramilitaries is so chaotic that it's no wonder that the U.S. press mostly ignores the growing mess. It's a lot easier to pontificate about the illegal immigrants and ignore the situation south of the border.

"From up here the bad guys are headquartered in Las Vegas, Phoenix and Albuquerque. The entrenched system is run by some long-time Colombian survivors, enjoying 'life in the United States' and wanting to maintain efficiency by simplifying their supply chain through Mexico. The two sides down there have a bloody history of fighting, making it messy for the *norteños*. Our indications are that rather than wait for the Mexicans to settle it, the guys up here will settle it for them."

"In other words, somebody is going to get killed."

"More likely a bunch of somebodies."

He stepped on the brakes and eased down the bank of a wash, then wobbled the steering wheel left and right on the upward climb to sidestep a couple of the bigger rocks that had become familiar over the years. "The narcotics rivalry in Mexico has been part of the background for years, just the same as the way the Mafia has been plagued by killings between families for decades. Now that the distribution on this side of the border has grown into a big business and merged with the money and arms smugglers, we've had to take notice."

\*\*\*\*

# Chapter Nine

Chester turned left onto a dirt road heading north, drove for another ten minutes. The road crossed another wash and then split in three directions. They continued to the right, across a flat area, a rutted track that curved around one of the mesas and then dipped through another arroyo and climbed up to the flat shoulder of the next plateau. A scattering of cottonwood trees marked the moist upwelling of the earth where Nez and Estrella had chosen to live. The hogan sat on the east side of the trees, door facing the sunrise, the earth in front of it sloping away toward the other mesas scattered under the flotilla of clouds that were slowly forming in the afternoon sky.

The hogan was carefully positioned on the southeast of the mesa so that during the winter months the sun warmed it all day, but during the summer the solar arc passed higher overhead and the mesa cast some cooling shade in the afternoons. Beyond the hogan, almost invisible behind the trees, sat a more modern prefab building — the "office hogan" — flanked by a solar panel and connected to a small satellite dish. Downslope, near a pole corral, Nez and Estrella were working under a brush arbor that scattered shade over their loom: a colorful octagon of wool like a giant spider web with art trapped in its tracings. Chester parked in the shade of the cottonwoods twenty yards back from the hogan and they waited, not only for the traditional Navajo politeness when arriving for a visit, but also so Nez and Estrella could reach a convenient place to tie off the weaving without randomly knotting the wool.

Estrella was the first to stand, then helped Nez to his feet. As Nez stood in the shade, Estrella came towards Tina, arms wide: "*Ya'at'eeh* and *biénvenidos, chica,*" she said, mixing the traditional Navajo and Mexican greetings. She was wearing a billowing skirt and a loose velvet blouse upon which shone a simple silver necklace of squash blossoms. The pendant, a dark blue oval of turquoise rimmed in silver, matched the barrette that pinned her bun to the top of her head. Tina smelled cinnamon when she hugged her grandmother...that meant fresh **móle**.

As Estrella went to hug her son, Tina stepped over under the ramada and gave her grandfather her usual French-style kiss on both cheeks. He seemed lean but solid to her, still maintaining his tall posture with just a trace of a stoop. The khakis he favored were faded, but soft and comfortable looking. His white hair still bristled in a "Marine" cut.

After the usual greetings and hugs, Nez pointed to the blanket circling from the center on the loom:

"A dream came to me. A long trail trodden by a wolf with a scorpion on its back..."

Tina looked closely at the pattern taking shape on the loom. Her grandparents had developed their own style, working on a spiral motif. Nez carrying on the Navajo weaving tradition, combining bands of color and contrast with the circular form of Estrella's Tohono O'odham basketry patterns. Instead of a traditional loom, Nez had crafted what looked more like a giant octagonal frame. The yarns as they radiated out from the center mingled reds, ochres, blacks and earth tones patterned into a twisting maze of zig-zags, diamond "dazzlers" and serpentine coils of color Nez liked to call "roads through the maze."

Usually intermingled into the geometric topography were Yeibechai and other traditional characters. ("But not Kokopelli" Estrella always insisted. "He's for stupid tourists.") Once when Tina had been about eight years old, her grandparents had given her a blanket with a pattern that looked suspiciously like Mickey Mouse ears. Nez had insisted with a twinkle in his eye that it was, in fact, "Mikichota" the spirit of deep sleep. She had always slept soundly when the blanket was draped over her by Mama or Papa as part of the end-of-day tuck ritual. The blanket still rested on her bed back in Washington, DC.

In the beginning, when they had been evacuated from Vietnam during the fall of Saigon, Mama and she had been brought to live here until Chester's discharge after the war's end. Not following the lessons learned by the French, the Vietnam War's futility had become undeniable to the U.S. and had finally been abandoned. As a girl, Tina had often helped grandmother Estrella mix the plant and mineral dyes for preparing the wool threads: *doot'izh*, the blue of sky; *izhin*, the black of night; *igai*, the white of dawn's first light in the east; and *itso*, the yellow of sunset in the west.

Each color would come with a story that Estrella would start: "Listen, girl, and I will tell you the O'odham story of how Elder Brother, I'itoi, was born to the earth and lives still in the caves and cliffs of Baboquivari Mountain down by Tucson."

Of course, when grandfather Nez was showing her how to twine the threads through the loom he would tell the same creation story, but in the Diné tradition with a completely different cast of characters.

The contrast in stories was more of a memory game for the six-year-old Tina than any source of confusion. She had already learned from Mama that the world had begun when King Lac Long Quan, the Dragon Lord of the Seas, married Princess Au Co, who had descended from the mountains and bore him 100 eggs, out of which 100 sons were born.

Looking back now as she studied the patterns taking shape on the loom, there had been little that could surprise a girl who already knew a world that could change from moist, green jungle and intermittent explosions, to this sprawling land of giants and boulders where sometime the wind stopped and there was no sound at all.

Many hours of looking out an airplane window between the contrasting landscapes had given her an ingrained sense of time, space and change. Mama's Buddha had expressed it best: everything was impermanent.

Now she looked at the intermingled bands of color and examined the creatures emerging from the wool: To the uninitiated eye, the blanket would look like yet another abstract masterpiece that had given Nez' and Estrella's creations an avid following in the art world and scattered them away to new homes in museums and collections around the world. But Tina could see, lurking under the spiral trail motif, the figure of Hadachishi, the DestroyerYe'i. The usual maze pattern that intermingled throughout her grandparents' work was this time jagged and irregular, instead of harmonious.

She searched for the traditional "door" or escape from the maze that was to allow the spirit of the piece to exit in *Himdag*, or harmony. She didn't see a door, but perhaps it was yet to be woven. Crawling up through the bottom of the maze from the southern direction, a grey wolf stalked, somehow sinister looking, even though, she reflected, it was merely a pattern of woven thread. Toward the center of the maze, seemingly ready to pounce, lurked a red and orange scorpion. The central section of the pattern was highlighted by streaks of lightning, but the source of the strikes seemed to be deep within, a very trompe-l'œil effect for a two dimensional work.

Tina reached out and ran her fingers over the scorpion and the wolf, the freshly spun wool soft and slick with lanolin under her fingertips. Despite the drama of the motif, the weaving was beautiful. She turned back to face her elders, who stood facing her in a row, Nez gripping a gnarled cane carved from an ironwood branch. The sun rolling low behind her cast a shadow over her family. As she began to walk toward them, Estrella said: "Come, girl, and we can steam the tamales I have prepared for your arrival."

When they reached the hogan, Estrella entered first. As Tina ducked to clear the door frame, she looked back and could see Chester and Nez silhouetted against the loom, surrounded by a circular web.

**\*\*\*\***

# Chapter Ten

Tina woke early the next morning and thought that when her shoulder felt better in a couple days she would collect wood to fire up the sweat lodge and fast. Certainly not to lose weight—her leathers told her when she wasn't being active enough to stay in shape. This would be her private ceremony for mental fitness, not vanity.

At the earliest light, Tina went out the door to join Estrella in the traditional Tohono O'odham "run to the sun" to start the day. It wasn't really a run. Estrella was almost 80 and Tina's broken collarbone made her breathing shallow and tentative. She slogged about 50 yards before turning back towards the base of the mesa.

Nearing the hogan, Tina rested on a rock, the rising sun warming her back. She watched Nez finish his traditional Navajo ritual: sprinkling the yellow corn pollen to greet the sun, then a series of yoga stretches he had learned from Mama Michelle when they had first escaped here from Vietnam.

The mix of cultural influences that wove through her family now reminded her of "The Many Words" a game she played with her mother. They would chatter through the list of names for a particular thing in every language they could think of.

When they got serious, they would compare more complex concepts, such as *Hozho,* the Navajo concept of beauty, balance, harmony that acts as a guide through life. In the Tohono O'odham tradition of grandmother Estrella, it was *Himdag,* a gift from the creator god I'itoi who lived in a cave below the peak of Baboquivari Mountain.

Mama Michelle would compare the whole-life concept of *Himdag* to Buddha's Middle Way taught to her by her Vietnamese mother and the straight and narrow of Christianity ascribed to by her French father.

Tina went back up the trail and joined her grandfather sitting on the plank bench in the arbor's shade. Layers of purple gray sky brightened to orange and finally faded to pink as the sun climbed up and gave them its first rays of the day.

"What are these thoughts on your brow, granddaughter," Nez asked.

"I was thinking of *Himdag, Hozho* and how much Jesus' 'straight and narrow' compares to Buddha's Middle Way."

"Maybe Jesus was a Buddhist," he said. "Or else he and Buddha were both excellent walkers."

She decided to egg him on and feigned seriousness: "That could be true. Jesus came after Buddha and would have had plenty of time to travel around and become exposed to the teachings. But how do you explain the huge similarities between the Middle Way and *Hozho* and *Himdag*. It's not that far fetched to see that the Tohono O'odham and the Dineh were close in time and place, but Buddhism was far away and in a different time.

"Maybe Buddha was a Navajo."

Laughter marked the end of her effort to keep a straight face. She remembered the many months spent here and in the "Scottsdale house" over the years. Wondered about how much of her grandfather's life she had only seen on the surface. As a girl she was familiar with him dressing up in his "lawyer suit," but knew little of what he had done when he was off her girlish radar.

She had been so excited when the code talkers were invited to Washington, DC, in 1992. She dragged Nez and Estrella to see the monuments. Nez asked to see the Vietnam Veterans wall. He went to the panel for 1967, guided by the slip of paper the volunteers at the top of the chevron had given him. He found the section, pointed to the name: "Begaye — one of the boys who wanted to be like us Code Talkers but got killed in the swamp."

After a day of walking and cab hopping, Tina realized from subtle clues that Nez knew his way around. How could she have been so dumb! He would tell the cabbie, "Turn right here…slow down…" A long look out the window as they passed a particular building, then "Drive on."

Now Tina saw clearly the connections between Nez and her father Chester and her own growing role, clearly far beyond a family tradition of mere government service. It was deeper, and more hidden, than she had suspected.

"You know what's happening, don't you grandfather? You've always known. I'm the one who is just finding out how things work."

He nodded. "Let's have breakfast and I'll tell you the story."

The way he told it: "When Victor left here with me to join the army, we did not know where were going, when, or if, would be coming back, and only had a vague idea of what we would be doing.

"The Pacific was a strange world, water flat as desert, but cold, wet and windy. Hawaii had black sand, volcanoes different from ours, and Polynesian and Asian faces. The Hawaiian people were much like us — tied to the land and traditions."

Chester Nimitz, it turned out, had kept Victor on his personal staff along with Nez:

"The first meeting I was in with my father, Admiral Nimitz and his staff, one second lieutenant complained that the meeting was supposed to be for officers and staff only.

"You went to Yale, didn't you son?" Nimitz asked.

"Yes sir," the guy answered proudly.

"Well that's great that you are such an expert on rules and regulations, but at Annapolis we learned that the most important thing in war is to win." Then he had that lieutenant hand over one of his sets of bars, he pinned them on Victor's collar and told the lieutenant to be in charge of writing up a battlefield commission for me, too. The guy never spoke at another meeting for the rest of the war. So here was your great-grandfather walking around with shiny double bars and me, a skinny kid just turned seventeen with lieutenant jay-gee on my collar and having to salute all these older sailors on deck."

He reached over and took a dip from the water bucket, held the ladle to his mouth and sipped, looking into the distance. Tina saw his eyes were clouded by age, but not by time.

"Nimitz had my father select a special group of men from his clan to be positioned shipboard during the Pacific campaign. The main operation was to pass signals and foil the Japanese attempts to interpret the messages." He gave her a sidelong glance as if balancing what level of "need to know" was pertinent and how much of the legend was family history she already knew. "The Code Talkers were primarily used for spontaneous radio encryption during the heat of battle. We were scattered among the units on the ground, as well as stationed shipboard to relay and send messages from the command structure. Nimitz liked that most of us were men of few words. He related to what many whites saw as our overly serious demeanor."

He dropped the ladle back into the bucket and leaned on his cane. "One day he talked with Victor and me about putting together an even smaller group within our overall structure. How many of the best and most trustful Code Talkers could my father assemble, he wanted to know. Since Preston Johnston and Major Jones had worked with my father to enlist the couple dozen earliest members, he was pretty familiar with them. They were, after all, mostly cousins or men with other close clan ties."

He tugged on the flap of his shirt pocket, as if adjusting invisible medals. "We settled on a dozen names. They were all flown to his carrier for a week of 'specialized training.' Then Nimitz had one of his personnel assistants assign them to the key battle groups with instructions to keep eyes and ears open around the top brass. We had been promoted to 'Code Listeners.' We were *Da-a-he-gi-ene,* the military term is liason, but for us it was "knows what others are doing.""

"Spy," Tina said.

Nez nodded. "You are carrying on the family tradition."

He gave her a long look. "Your father was certain you would be more like your mother and gravitate toward the diplomatic level, but you surprised him when you wanted to become a Marine."

"And it surprised mama, too," she blushed.

"Must just be khaki blood," he smiled. He looked back out at the horizon and the distant past. "I got to fly quite a bit between carriers the rest of the war. Victor was nervous enough being out in the ocean, so he stayed pretty much at Nimitz' side.

"I got the sailor's tour of the Western Pacific: Tarawa, Saipan, Okinawa, Tinian, the Ryuku Islands, Mariana Islands and of course, Iwo Jima. Unfortunately, the welcomes were warm, mostly machine gun fire."

He stood, grabbed his cane and started walking toward the office hogan. "I'll show you the book."

The inside of the trailer was cool, but Tina guessed it was more for the functioning of the electronics. Nez was as happy in the heat as a lizard. He pulled a dark leather bound scrapbook off the shelf and they sat together at the table as he leafed through and pointed to a photo labeled: "Fleet Admiral Chester W. Nimitz, USN, signs the Instrument of Surrender as United States Representative, on board USS Missouri (BB-63), 2 September 1945."

Standing directly behind him were General Douglas MacArthur, Admiral William F. Halsey and a flotilla of navy officers. Nez pointed to a spot in the background: "These little heads are your great-grandfather Victor Toledo and me."

He leafed silently through a few more photos: somber Japanese officials in top hats signing their country's fate, cratered island landscapes of the Pacific, ruined cities in Japan.

"After the surrender signing I figured that was it, the war was over, but Nimitz asked us if we would consider coming with him to Washington, DC. Victor had no one to return home to, so he agreed. I was eager to get back to Tucson and find Estrella, so Nimitz made sure I got fast-tracked on the GI Bill for the University of Arizona. After Estrella and I got married and your daddy was born, I decided to name him after Chester."

He stood and put the book on the shelf. "That's enough for today. You can R&R after lunch with a little light weaving and tomorrow I'll tell you how I caught up with Victor in Washington."

As she got up from the table, Tina felt the room tilt slightly. She put her left hand on the table to steady herself and got a reminder from the collarbone that she was still healing from the motorcycle crash.

Nez was watching her: "Estrella will tell you it's siesta time after lunch. You can skip weaving until tomorrow."

"*Entiendo,*" she smiled.

\*\*\*\*

# Chapter 11

The second morning, Tina decided to take a walk on the spiral trail that circled up the mesa. She was able to climb only halfway to the top and picked a spot to rest on along the shady west side of the trail.

She sat in a hollow weathered into the rock, her back against the cool sandstone. She rested quietly, looking out into forever, the sun filling her eyes as it crept over the top and began warming her perch. She was beyond alert. Everything lived, moved, died in a light and time wider than a hawk soaring in the heavens. Without words she knew this was *hozho, Himdag,* the balance of "now" that so many chased, not knowing that the chasing was the problem.

An old fable bubbled in her memory: The student coming to the master with the question "If you had a magic lamp that would grant you any wish, what would you wish for?" To which the master answered: "To stop wishing."

…and do what needs to be done. Her mind relaxed, volition melted in the afternoon sun. Memories flowed like water: the jungle and sweet floral aromas of her childhood, the black and white outfits of the Saigon nuns, lessons absorbed in French, Vietnamese, Navajo and English.

Then the long plane ride to America and a bus to Arizona. The mesas stretched before her now, dappled by the scattered clouds, timeless backdrops that brought memories of learning Spanish and Tohono O'odham from Grandmother Estrella.

Eventually Papa came home and they took another long plane ride, this time to Washington, DC, and a maze of buildings filled with "history," though none could compare with the history she had already seen in the timeless desert, Monument Valley and the Grand Canyon.

But soon she discovered more languages! Washington was filled with them, and even more so New York, where Mama often took her while Papa was assigned there doing something they called "bureaucrat work." New York was a hive of languages, the streets a spinning radio dial of overheard conversations.

Finally she had discovered the most glorious, the sweetest of all the languages: mathematics. What an infinite universe of geometry, physics, relativity. After astrophysics, learning computer languages was like going back to kindergarten.

The symbols that add, subtract, multiply and divide opened the door to a panoply of equations. Pi, theta, phi held sway across the universe — way more than identifiers for fraternities or her little key from phi beta kappa. Sweet delta, the little triangle a symbol of change, as Buddhist a symbol as ever there was. As were entropy and reversion to the norm.

And Zeta, the Z, "zed," the end. Now Grupo Zeta — the bad guys. She hadn't an iota of a clue where that trail would lead. She dozed for a bit, woke up thirsty. She sipped from the canteen in her fanny pack, then stood slowly, letting her circulation equalize. Good, no dizziness.

She'd told Estrella she would cook tonight. Michelle had packed ingredients for *bun thit nuong,* vermicelli noodles over a bed of greens, sliced cucumber, sprouts and topped with chopped goodies. Tina's personal touch was to use pepperoni and fresh mozzarella. Despite the Italian twist, she knew in advance that her grandfather's ancient joke would be repeated: "What, Vietnamese food again?"

\*\*\*\*

# Chapter 12

Day three, Wednesday, "water man day." As a girl, Tina
had always looked forward to the arrival of the big van. Two
burly men would help Nez load barrels onto the platform
behind the office hogan, talk with him in low voices for a few
minutes and leave behind a large parcel. The parcel always
included a packet of letters from Vietnam for Michelle and a
treat for Tina.

Whenever Nez would leave for a week or two, he would
kiss her goodbye and say he was going to "work for the water
man."

Today she sat under the brush arbor and watched the van
roll into view. The current van was newer, but the subtle
coloration made it blend, not so much into the landscape, but
into forgetfulness. From one side it appeared dusty green, on
the other side blue. Undertones of brown and gray overlaid
the paint job to the extent that you couldn't really pin down a
color depending on whether you saw it coming or going. A
few artfully placed dents and patches of "rust" completed the
subterfuge. A close look at the official looking logo on the
door showed it to be undecipherable.

The license was no clue: "WTR MN" vanity plates that
weren't traceable through the Arizona registry. She had tried
once, just for a laugh. No hit. Now she was working for the
water man, too.

The routine was unchanged: A couple of empty barrels lowered easily to the ground, the two full ones rolled up the ramp by a pair of young muscle boys, neither of whom looked Navajo, their cowboy hats contrasting with the short haircuts and aviator sunglasses. Then a large parcel was carried into the office and after ten minutes the crew reappeared, got in the van and rolled away with hardly a puff of dust to mark their trail.

After the van left, Tina helped Estrella with spooling some new yarn, freshly died a deep blue, almost black.

Estrella said the blue was for a "crazy maze" that Nez planned to overlay throughout the current pattern. "Crazy maze, that's almost like our life, *entiende?*"

Tina nodded her assent. She and her parents certainly were carrying on the worldly roller coaster that had begun decades ago.

"Nez was a boy when I first saw him down in Tucson," Estrella reminisced, looking at her husband as he came toward them. "But he came back from the Pacific a man, and changed. He was happy to be home in Arizona, but would constantly tell stories of exotic lands. He thought the cities of Japan were more beautiful than anything he had seen here."

She and Tina looked at Nez, their silence providing an invitation for his comment: "The buildings were carved wood and looked like sculptures or huge wedding cakes."

He picked up a tiny shuttle, threaded a bit of blue yarn through the hole, sat on the low bench and began poking the needle through the front of the rug. Estrella sat behind the loom and pulled the yarn taught before sending it back through to Nez for the next stitch.

"Admiral Nimitz saw the damage to Japan and was determined that America should help the country rebuild. He didn't want the Japanese to become a downtrodden people the way Germany had been treated after WWI. I wasn't privy to much of what he and my father talked about, since I was out hopping the islands, but I think Nimitz relied on Victor as a sounding board for what it was like to be a member of a downtrodden people. Navajos aren't big on revenge and Nimitz liked that."

He pulled the blue yarn tight, then picked up a second shuttle threaded with red, twisted the two yarns in a spiral and sent the two shuttles back through to Estrella.

"Nimitz also agreed to help President Truman start scaling back the navy. That was a tougher assignment than rebuilding Japan. Many officers didn't want to be cashiered out of the service after having tasted power. Victor and his small group of listeners started out behind the scenes as expeditors, but as Truman got to know them, several more like-minded officers and civilians were added to the group."

Nez switched to an alternating pattern of black and white yarn. Tina looked at the rug and began to notice that the traces winding through the work were small, but added a subtle depth to the overall piece. She wondered how such a vision evolved.

"Grandfather, you said you had a dream about the wolf and the scorpion. Did you see this pattern in the dream?"

He smiled. "Much like the trails of life, you start in a direction and don't know where you will end up. Victor found that out when he decided to stick with this group that was evolving and later found out that he was close to the center of it."

His fingers danced over the loom now, weaving copper wire from a spool in and out of the pattern and pinching each wire end with a small turquoise bead. "Everyone involved had kept their day jobs and moved up their respective ladders. It hadn't started as a secret agency, it wasn't an agency at all. It was really more a way to communicate behind the scenes about what was really going on and trade goals to move toward a certain outcome."

"How did they get you hooked up all the way out here in Arizona?"

"I had met the Udall brothers when Estrella and I were going to the University of Arizona. They were a couple years ahead of me. I had run into them at the law library, seen them at the debates, but I think the first time they took notice of me was when our Indian-Mexican basketball team whupped their butts in a summer league tournament."

He straightened up, as if the memory made him stretch for the basket in his mind. "Those Udall boys were nuts about basketball. Morris had even played for a year as a pro with the Denver Nuggets after he graduated from the U of A."

He paused, held out his hand and Tina passed him a cup of water from the jar. He sipped, then broke into a broad smile. "I had heard that Mo had a glass eye and that was why he had given up pro basketball and come back to law school. So our team would holler out our plays in Navajo and work the ball toward his bad eye and make him spin to keep the play in sight. Got him plenty dizzy. Forced him into awkward directions when we were on defense, too."

He took another sip. "We kept hollering and they didn't know what we were saying. Plus it didn't hurt that we had some pretty tall Navajos who could shoot. A couple of us had spent time on the carriers with nothing much better to do than to play hoops. We only beat them by a couple points, but it was quite a surprise to them.

"After the game, I shook Mo's hand and said 'I guess we blind-sided you.' He gave me a strange look and then busted out laughing. A couple years later I graduated and started working at his law office.

"By then, older brother Stewart had started the climb up the political ladder, from school board to U.S. House, then Kennedy tapped him to be Secretary of Interior. Mo was elected to fill Stu's seat in Congress, and there I was, a Navajo lawyer involved with big environmental issues affecting Arizona, and about to get sucked into one of the most challenging eras of our history."

He drained the cup and handed it back to Tina.

"Eisenhower had managed to keep J. Edgar Hoover at arm's length, but the Kennedys didn't like the FBI's strong arm tactics and dirt digging.

"Tensions worldwide were ratcheting up: Gary Powers was shot down in a U-2 spy plane over Russia, holes were being dug out here in Arizona to house Titan missile silos, the Vietnam war was heating up. Bobby started going after organized crime.

"JFK hit the boiling point on the CIA after the Bay of Pigs fiasco and the mess with the assassination of South Vietnam's dictator Ngo Diem. Three weeks later the president himself was assassinated."

Nez snipped the last bit of copper wire, crimped a bead and stood to take a look.

"Good intentions can get snarled, too. In the middle of the night after Dallas, while Lyndon Johnson was taking the oath on the Bible, Bobby Kennedy huddled with a handful of the key cabinet members, including Stu Udall and told them to go deep, stay deep, stay secret.

"Udall brought me in to help Victor and the rest. The group also got a boost from Hubert Humphrey who bridled under Johnson's threat to scuttle Humphrey's candidacy if he didn't stay on the boat in favor of the Vietnam War."

Nez picked up his cane and pointed to a series of bright spots that now glowed a copper highlight against the depth of the background. "Order among chaos, wouldn't you say?"

"I'll bring out some sandwiches," Estrella said and headed for the hogan. Victor watched her go.

"You grandmother wasn't happy about going to Washington, but she had connected with educational issues for Dineh, Tohono O'odham and other tribal schools in Arizona. Stu and Mo got her situated at a good crossroads between federal agencies and she took right to it. Of course, she insisted on having a break from the Washington winters, so we spent a lot of time at the Scottsdale house and out here at the hogan."

Tina looked at the satellite dish and antennas atop the office hogan. "But you kept in touch with the water man."

"We were swimming in it. Victor was past 60 and ready to spend more time here, so he became our background choreographer as we sorted out who could be trusted.

"There were plenty of backs being stabbed. I think President Truman had it right when he said, 'If you want a friend in Washington, get a dog.'"

\*\*\*\*

# Chapter 13

Day four: Tina woke before dawn after tossing restlessly most of the night. The package from the water man had included another briefing for her: a complete rundown on the arms shipment intercept and Ruben's murder.

She had torn each page to bits after reading, and now lit a match to the pile in the outdoor fire pit. Even the smell of the paper seemed foul, so she added a few broken pieces of mesquite kindling and let the scented flames purify into ashes.

She filled her canteen, left a note for Nez and Estrella and set out in the pre-dawn gray toward the trail up the mesa. Despite the restless night, her head felt good this morning and the dull ache in her shoulder was hardly noticeable. The moon was setting to the west as she started uphill.

After a half hour, she had warmed up and reached the northern side of the mesa. The trail, while technically an upward spiral around the whole mesa, took what nature gave, rising and falling to match the jagged contour eroded into the face of the rock.

A few more minutes and she slowed to ease her way across a loose pile of scree that marked a huge crack down the northeast face. Her strength was returning, but she didn't trust her balance completely yet and wanted to avoid sliding down the chute and getting banged up again.

The sun pipped the horizon as she made it across the twenty yards of tiptoeing and scrambling. This was far enough for today. She sat and looked out toward the procession of rocky mesas, chimneys, spikes, mounds and mountains that marked the interplay of rock, sky and weather in the Four Corners. Tomorrow she would make it to the top, but for now she would let time flow without her for a while.

The news about Ruben had flown at her like arrows over the past couple days: ears to brain, head to heart, tears to eyes.

She would live today, most likely tomorrow. Ruben's todays were done. She wasn't sure how many tomorrows she had left, but avenging his death and restoring balance was now her way. This was not merely revenge, but a reinstatement of justice. She suspected it would be a lifelong path as it had been for Nez, Estrella, Chester and Michelle.

And Victor before them. The family's link to Ruben had its roots in a long-ago detour, out in the Pacific. There had always been talk of "the sailor who didn't come home." That legacy finally came full circle during Tina's freshman year as a midshipman at Annapolis.

She had spotted the giant watching her every Tuesday as she double-timed across the square in front of Bancroft Hall heading for her calculus class. She knew who he was: There were even rumors of a Heisman Trophy for Ruben Mataia Gonzales, star fullback for the midshipmen, the hottest player since Roger Staubach, class of '65.

It wasn't unusual for Tina to catch glances or outright stares from upperclassmen, but today it was Ruben who singled her out: "Halt, Swab."

She stomped to attention, "Yes, Sir!"

He was giving her the once-over and she gave him the benefit of the doubt that he was checking her name tag instead of catching a gratuitous look at her breasts.

"I used to know some Toledo boys. Where are you from, Swab?"

"Sir! I am from Arizona."

"And you are?"

"Sir! Midshipman Fourth Class Valentina Toledo, sir!"

The smile that barely lifted his upper lip gave him a serene look, a fleshy Samoan Buddha.

"Arizona's as big as New England; where exactly are you from, Swab? Phoenix, Tucson, Payson? Flagstaff, Coolidge, Florence? Or maybe a small town like Gila Bend or Eloy…where exactly Swab?

Surprise added to her confusion at the awkward confrontation. How would a Samoan midshipman know so much about Arizona?

"Sir, my family is from the Navajo reservation – a small town called Teas Toh."

Most surprising, he then addressed her in Navajo: "You should run to class or you will be late. Dismissed."

"Sir, thank you sir!"

It would take several phrases in many of her languages to describe the dismay she had felt when he had started talking to her in diné.

Two weeks later he stopped her again, hollered loudly about the state of her uniform, the necessity of courtesy to upperclassmen, the fact that swabs were the lowest form of life.

In diné he whispered, "Stand at attention so it doesn't look like we're fraternizing."

"Sir, yes sir!" She pulled her shoulders back even farther, catching admiring glances from a couple other upperclassmen passing by. He gave her coordinates and a rendezvous time.

Ruben looked Samoan, but, in fact, had a Code Talker grandfather, too, who went back to the South Pacific to live out his life after WWII.

"So that makes me one-quarter Navajo," he explained that night during a quieter meeting in a study room at the Nimitz Library. His strong Navajo nose cut the Polynesian face like a dull hatchet. He had been appointed to Annapolis with the goal of playing football — several of his cousins had made it to the NFL.

His grandfather, it turned out, was Ahiga Begaye Toledo, a cousin of Tina's great grandfather Victor. After the war, Ahiga had traded the desert for the sea and worked his way around the Pacific before settling in Satupaitea, Savai'i, Western Samoa.

He hadn't intended to settle, but he had met and married a Samoan woman Ferukia Mataia, who was worth staying home for.

"She bore him five strong sons," Ruben told Tina. "Then my mother, Petania, rounded out the family." He winked on the "rounded." The football program listed him at 6-4, 240.

"Those boys were kings of the island at sports. They got the nickname the 'Toledo Tornados.'"

"As for my mom, she was a looker. Married a sailor from Mexico when she was 19 and had me. Then he got himself drowned on one of the tuna boats and my five uncles took over teaching me the guy stuff. My uncle Notah always used to tell his brothers, "Look at this kid. We taught him everything we know and he still don't know nothing.'"

Tina envied him the extended Samoan family. Chester was an only son, and she...well, she was here at Annapolis.

Fall was coming early, so Ruben wore his letterman's jacket, studded with a layer of pins atop the athletic letters. Tina noticed his senior class ring was set with a deep blue chunk of turquoise.

Ruben saw her looking at it: "My grandfather Ahiga Toledo died when I was nine, but he told me stories about the big mountains in Arizona and the red sunsets and the blue stones."

"How did your mixed heritage go over on the island?"

"*No problemo.* Sailors had either been washing ashore or jumping ship for hundreds of years. Maybe it was the beautiful Samoan women."

Tina could tell from his laugh that she was blushing. She wanted to joke back somehow, but he was still an upperclassman and they hadn't yet ironed out their complete clan linkage as passed through the Navajo sides of their families.

"Samoans like to joke with each other, Navajo girl. Don't worry about it." He was speaking his rusty Navajo now. "My uncles said that with my Navajo and Mexican blood, that made me a Navameximoan, which was why I was so good at sports. Said I wasn't as big as my pure Samoan teammates, so I had to play twice as hard."

Tina told him about her Mexican roots, too, through grandmother Estrella, then about papa Chester marrying a French/Vietnamese woman.

"Those Toledo boys must have a taste for exotic women," he kidded her. She knew she was blushing, but she also knew now it was safe with him.

Today, looking out at the Arizona landscape, Tina held those memories of Ruben, pushed away the images of his corpse unceremoniously dumped in Tucson. She would find his killer for justice, but if there was a chance that bringing that justice entailed punishment, she was ready to dole it out. Just the way Ruben doled out punishment by the yard that football season, mowing down tacklers with strength and agility. Plus a couple of sumo moves he had picked up from his uncles.

They hadn't been able to continue their geneology tracking until after football season. That particular week of their first long chat had been during the run-up to the Army game. In order to prevent the usual inter-service mascot kidnapping, the Annapolis midshipmen corps moved Bill the Goat into Ruben's room, correctly figuring that there was no way anybody would want to take him, Ruben, on.

Unfortunately, Bill had given Ruben a stout butt in the knee, slightly twisting it. Late in the game that weekend, Ruben had made a cut through the line to score his fourth touchdown, but in the pileup in the end zone, he had felt a pop. That put an end to the Heisman hopes, but Navy beat Army 37-10.

Ruben wasn't crazy about languages the way Tina was, but they were both fluent in Spanish, and she helped him catch back up with his rusty Navajo. They spoke English when other midshipmen were around.

In exchange for the Navajo coaching, Ruben taught her the art of *su'ifefiloi* — a mixing of English and Samoan through prose and poetry.

They also tried to sort out the distant clan ties, which made them remote cousins. Tina visualized it almost mathematically as third cousins depending on the degrees of exogamy and consanguinity, complicated by the contrasting kinship traditions of the Polynesians and Uto-Aztecans. Ruben stuck with "distant cousins."

He said she was *"tausonga."*

All Samoan ancestors of three generations or more upstream are termed *tupunga,* not *tupuna,* the term for grandparent. All descendants of two generations or more after a particular individual are termed *makupuna.*

The participle uso, which in Samoa means sibling of the same sex as the speaker, is used as a term embracing all one's closer collateral relatives, aunts, uncles, and cousins. *Tausonga,* which in Samoa means sibling of the opposite sex to the speaker, refers only to the distant relatives of one's kinship group, irrespective of generation. The meaning of "close" and "distant" in the terms uso and tausonga made Tina compare the "born to" and "born for" lineage description in Navajo. When she began to add in Vietnamese traditions with remote links to the tall Hmong mountain people, Rubens eyes glazed over and he kidded her in a mock southern accent: "Sounds like we're kinfolk, y'all."

It all went back to the Code Talkers. They shared *tupunga* — distant ancestors — and were *tausonga,* opposite sex. "Tausonga Tina" became one word Tausongatina…which had a nice ring to it in his Samoan accent.

Eventually, he called her "T" for *tausonga,* Tina and Toledo.

As for Tina, she came to honor, admire and respect him so much that she always felt more comfortable calling him "Sir." Since he was three years ahead of her at Annapolis, he always stayed a rank above her later on in the Marine Corps, so the tradition stuck.

Now the tradition, and his memory, had slipped into the past, and Tina once again was face to face with the reality of impermanence. The philosophical Buddhist concept had become real to her even as a little girl in Saigon. She had seen her first dead bodies in the chaos of the streets as Michelle had dragged her to the rendezvous point for the helicopter airlift. That first feeling in the chopper, the upward turning senses of lightness and looking down as the world dropped away had stayed with her, marked her path to helicopter training in the Marines and her first assignment in the Purple Foxes, flying CH-46 Sea Knight transport helicopters.

Ruben had taken his last flight, home to Samoa in a flag draped casket. Tina took a deep cleansing breath, stood and stretched for a few minutes before beginning her hike back down the mesa.

When she returned to the arbor, Nez and Estrella were finishing up the day's weaving. The piece looked almost finished to Tina, but she realized once again that the maze did not have a door. She traced her finger around the periphery, savored the colors and smell of the wool as Estrella toted the basket of yarns toward the hogan.

Taking a step back, she noticed that the spirals could vaguely be seen as a yin-yang, but that the balance was slightly off. Her artistic sense was that there was a tension or dynamism because of this, but that the overall feel was much less harmonious than she had come to expect from her grandparents' works.

"I have a question, my grandfather," she said, moving to his side on the smooth plank bench.

"Again?"

She smiled at his gentle humor. How many questions had she posed to him in this exact place over the past three decades? The bench was as much a focal point of the homestead as the hogan. Many times they had spent an afternoon spinning, dying and weaving the wool, turning the gift of the sheep into their own gift of art.

She knew as a girl that grandfather had been a soldier, just like Papa, but that he had retired. The new building came years later, and the two men spent plenty of time in there during her family's visits from their new home in Washington. When she had been allowed in, she had seen the fancy radios and typewriters that typed by themselves. She was too old by then to believe in magic, but old enough to know about secrets.

Sitting on the bench today, looking out at a panorama that stretched to forever, Tina felt the easiness of home twinged with just a trace of foreboding. That intuition shaped her question: "Why is there no *dau* in the maze?" She used the Tohono O'odham word for the exit that traditionally led from the maze to the world outside.

He pondered for a minute, not a long time by Navajo standards, stood and walked over to the loom.

"I told you about my dream. The wolf came first in my dream. It had been walking a long time. It is walking now; perhaps it will be on its journey forever."

He gave her a look of contemplation, as if weighing how many layers of dream he should share.

"The scorpion was following the wolf. It has also been following a long time. Unless policies or situations on both sides of the border change, the scorpion may follow forever and not find a *dau*. I left it to find its own way out."

The direct reference to the real world as opposed to the metaphor of dream startled Tina.

"You know about my mission?"

"I can hear a long way from this place."

She realized that he had been in at the beginning, that she was just now approaching the *dau* herself, that the door into the maze would lead to a trail that would change her life. Be her life.

**\*\*\*\***

# Chapter 14

Day five. The spiral trail would be hers today. The scramble across the scree was little more than a speed bump. Walking mindfully, Tina breathed the cool morning air and enjoyed a clear head, no dizziness and a complete sense of returning strength.

Even the deepest breaths flowed without pain. When she reached the top of the mesa it was like returning to the home of an old friend. She held her arms to the risen sun and sang a small chant, a simple melody with the words "thank you" in many languages, accompanied by a spinning combination of slow stretches that evolved into a *tai chi kata* culminating in a few explosive kicks that had served her well in close quarters.

The top of the mesa encompassed about eight acres. The hard basalt layer acted as a cap and as the eons eroded the sandstone underneath, the traditional top hat shape evolved. It would have been a perfect helicopter landing pad: treeless, flat and with 360-degree visibility.

Sweat glistened on her brow as she walked over to the largest rock on the mesa, a rectangular mass the size of a refrigerator, which had resisted nature's attempts to crumble it. She rested for a minute, leaning against the shady west side, rolling her neck, testing the collarbone.

Having savored the coolness, she walked around to the other side and sat on a smaller stone, eyes closed against the sun, and enjoyed the warmth. She unbuttoned her shirt and dropped it on the ground, enjoying the heat on her breasts. She looked at the two loops of the collarbone brace: the white straps stood out against the tan of her skin like a shoulder holster. She undid the Velcro, slipped off the brace and closed her eyes again.

Slowly she stretched without the brace, easing into a full extension of her arms in every direction. *Recovery complete; time to go operational.*

Back on with the shirt, a bandana from her pocket wrapped around her head, and the brace stuffed in her fanny pack, Tina took a sip from her canteen and walked over to the lowest spot on the mesa top. Winds and rains had deposited a layer of sand across an area the size of a basketball court. She walked around from the sandy patch in a widening spiral and began carrying back rocks of all sizes and sorted them into piles in the center.

Then a sip from the canteen, deep breath, mind stilled. In the sand, Tina began to draw I'itoi's maze, the twists and turns symbolic of the changes and choices of a life. First, she used a pointed shard of basalt to scribe an open circle about ten meters in the sand. In the opening at the top of the circle, the *dau*, she drew a little stick figure of I'itoi himself, the Man in the Maze. From the door, the path of the maze went down to the middle, then turned and went to the edge of the circle and traced a path inside the perimeter, then turned again and made another circular loop. This was not like the typical white man's maze of numerous dead ends and only one successful path to the exit. I'itoi's maze had one entrance, several circular turnings, and always ended in the center.

This was the maze of life, Tina mused, once again enraptured by the drawing process. At each stage or passage, whether we know it or not, we can look back at what we have done, but then we make the choice to take a turn and continue the journey. At the center, we have one last chance to look back on our choices and paths before the Sun God blesses us and welcomes us to the next world.

As she thought deeply about the twists that had brought her to this place in her life, including Ruben's horrible death, Tina pondered the patterns of history that ran through her family and the threads that connected to form a quest against wars, injustice and violence. The suns that rose and set across the ancient landscape that surrounded her made her want to call back across time to her ancestors and chant that although they were gone, their dreams and hopes lived on through her. She spread her hands to the horizon and looked with a gaze that knew no boundaries.

With a small, melodic chant, she began to gather rocks smoothed by the eons of winds across the mesas. Her mind drifted with the task as the sun climber straight overhead.

Now she arranged the dark of the rocks carefully along the sandy lines of the maze, their solidity and shadow putting the path into even starker contrast. This must have been how the tradition of Navajo sand paintings began in the depths of history — tracing the spirit world into symbolism with the materials at hand. Then the painting swept away, impermanent. Maybe grandfather was right. Maybe Buddha was a Navajo.

As her convoluted spiral reached the end, Tina walked around the perimeter of the mesa, looking for just the right round stone to place in the center of the maze. As she picked the stone up, a tiny red scorpion darted away.

****

# Chapter 15

On the way down the trail, Tina saw a wisp of dust in the distance marking papa's truck coming to pick her up.

When she reached the hogan, she joined them at a picnic table for Estrella's "lunch for the road." After the goodbye hugs, Tina took one last look at the rug stretched on the loom, running her fingers along the maze. She would be tracing a maze of murder, not knowing where the twists would lead.

As soon as they hit the paved road, papa pointed to the glove box. She opened it to find a paper bag of fresh croissants. Nestled under the bag she found a slim envelope. She opened it, pulled out an ID badge printed with her most current photo, a bar code and a shiny embedded chip — but no name; three passports with different names; and a velvet pouch with … the knife.

She laid it on the velvet and held it in both palms, the Japanese characters glinting in the sun: 您 您 Tina's spoken Japanese was more fluent than her reading of the more than 5,000 kanji, but she knew the symbols on the fragment meant "rain water." There was no one alive to tell what had been said on the rest of the samurai sword's inscription.

She looked at her father, who was maintaining a calm focus on the road ahead. "I guess my R&R is over." She slipped the ID badge around her neck.

"Your password is your six-digit birthday," he said. "We have plenty of opportunity for fancier passkeys when you start sorting through the bank codings."

"What bank codings?"

He gave her a sly smile. "International routing numbers, my daughter. You are about to become one of the top money launderers in the world. I know you are as good with numbers as you are with words, so you can ease back into the mix with a thorough debriefing. I have a nice quiet place we're going where you can study the topography of the road ahead. There's a nasty cast of characters to deal with and you'll need to be able to play your part without a script. In the meantime, here's what we've learned so far."

He pointed again to the glove box. Another fat folder, flap sealed with the wax maze imprint, had a report on the explosive aftermath of Vegetable Man and his cohorts. Tina digested the background as they rolled south toward Phoenix.

The semi-trucks had sliding door panels built into the sides of their trailers. The drivers could pull alongside similar trucks and load cargo from the other trailer rig without using the highly visible doors in back.

The first connection in Fort Huachuca had been a swap of cocaine and cash for the shoulder-fired missiles. Tina had guessed that the guy in camo had been paying the cash, her thinking at the time was that it was a straight drug buy. In fact, according to the deathbed interview with Vegetable Man, the first stop had been only a partial cargo swap. Ten missiles had been loaded aboard in exchange for the cocaine and cash, the transfer of cargos expedited with a pallet jack aboard the drug truck.

The second swap had taken longer because the cargos had been bulkier. Vegetable Man offloaded several tons of marijuana distributed among the four other trucks. In return, several hundred semiautomatic assault rifles, grenades, plastic explosives and cases of ammunition.

Tina dozed a bit on the way back, waking when her father turned off the freeway at Sky Harbor Airport. They both showed identification at the security gate and drove along the hangars that housed the private planes. As they approached a hangar, Chester pushed a button on the door opener clipped to his visor. The hangar door lifted to reveal a sleek little eight-passenger plane with twin jets on its tail. Courtesy of Uncle Sam, Tina assumed. The two-man crew nodded at them from behind dark glasses as they climbed the stairs and nestled in the back of the cabin

The plane climbed out heading northwest, over the red jewel of Taliesin West, Frank Lloyd Wright's architectural laboratory, then circled around the backside of the jagged Superstition Mountains. Dreams of gold lay buried deep in those rocks, along with many scattered bones of would-be miners who had vanished in the rugged spine. The splotches of green from the golf courses that dotted the freeway south of the mountains symbolized the new gold rush: creeping suburbanization that had turned Phoenix and the Valley of the Sun into another Los Angeles, minus the ocean.

As they flew, Papa briefed her about the growing violence between the eastern and western factions of the Mexican gangs. The increased American border enforcement had created unexpected problems for the Border Patrol and other federal agencies. New drug and human smuggling routes snaked through Arizona, now complicated by coyote battles on a growing scale, and organized clashes targeting law enforcement on both sides of the border.

"Our most dangerous players are an American narco gang called Mara Salvatrucha," her father said. "They want to battle the Mexican lords for distribution, or worse, cooperate to consolidate them, take over pipelines through Las Vegas, Phoenix and Albuquerque. From there, it's like any other interstate business. Three tectonic plates pushing from different directions — the earthquake will be ugly. Chopping off the head of snake may make it grow another head, but even if we only buy a few years at a time, it's worth the price.

"The worst mutation of all this is the growing frequency of direct attacks on the Mexican government, and now it's spilling over the border into the U.S. It's beyond just a bunch of cops and robbers with the bad guys shooting to make a getaway. Armed convoys of criminals with assault rifles, grenades and rocket launchers have been attacking police stations, lobbing grenades and openly threatening journalists or officials who call for more enforcement."

The jet leveled off over the cages of the State Prison in Florence, then circled around the west side of the Rincon Mountains that marked the edge of the Tucson valley. Sunset glinted off the wings of thousands of mothballed airplanes as the pilot entered the glide path for a landing at Davis-Monthan Air Force Base. This was the official "boneyard" of the nation's military planes when they were taken out of service.

Miles of aluminum carcasses gleamed in orderly rows, sparkling in the late afternoon sun. Some looked grisly in ritual dismemberment: One whole section of desert contained nothing but B-52s, their severed wings strewn on either side of the fuselages so Russian satellites could verify their decay as part of the SALT disarmament treaty.

As they made their final approach, Tina looked down on the Pima Air Museum, a famous side effect of the airframe salvage and recycling mission at D-M. Vintage planes from virtually every era constituted an air force of history: Her favorite was the "pregnant guppy" that had been used to transport the X-15.

As the runway rose to meet them, it seemed odd to Tina that she had heard no radio traffic or chatter from the cockpit. The plane taxied across a runway far from the control tower, approaching a separate compound surrounded by it's own security fence. A gate glided open and the plane rolled into an unmarked hangar and came to a stop next to a sleek four-seat jet helicopter. She recognized it as one of the new Eurocopters, but wasn't sure of the model. What she was sure of was that it was private and very expensive. The dark blue paint was unblemished by identification.

She looked at her father, but he simply smiled and motioned her to board it. The two-man crew rolled the chopper out of the hangar, clicked through their preflight checklist, and started the high-pitched turbine.

As the helicopter took off into the settling darkness, Tina noticed that in addition to radio silence, this trip was being flown without lights.

"There's another big badass trying to move into the mix," her father continued. "His name is Jackson Truong. He's grown from Saigon, through Hong Kong and into Canada by way of Vancouver when the British let the Chinese take over in Hong Kong.

"He's left a trail of bodies behind him as he's followed the flow of cash. Most recently, he's stepped on the toes of the Asian Boyz as he's moved south through California.

"What we know so far: Born 1973, mother a Saigon prostitute, father's name unknown, but she saw the baby was black so named him after the only black soldier she had slept with. She'd seen the Jackson tag on his fatigues."

The pilots were flying low, dark, in radio silence, and again off the direct route, along the backside of the Santa Rita Mountains. Tina could tell they were skirting Fort Huachuca, flying barely above the tree line through the saddle between Mount Hopkins and Mount Graham. She was on the left side, so she could see the Whipple Observatory atop Mount Hopkins glowing a ghostly white as the stars began to shine.

"Do you think this Jackson was involved with Ruben's murder?"

He nodded. "From what we know the guy has an ax to grind. He grew up as a street kid in Saigon, and being black meant he got the worst treatment when the Communists moved back in. Crime has been his life and he is very good at it, and very brutal. He hates Americans, and is rumored to have killed several black prostitutes since he infiltrated to the U.S."

The helicopter skimmed over open rangeland at the base of the mountains. A shallow valley sloped toward the Santa Cruz River and Tina could see in the distance the huge man-made mesas left by the tailing piles of the open pit copper mines.

"Truong has also been buddied up with the crooked side of the military wherever he's gone," her father continued. "In Vietnam and China, that helped expand his drug trafficking business. He has this odd hobby of liking to go on strafing runs in helicopters. So far he has stuck to inanimate targets — like stretches of forest in Canada and a series of junked cars he had plopped in the desert north of Kingman.

"Word is he can fly, but prefers to sit in the gunnery seat and blast away. That could be a vicious habit if he tries to take out his competition along the border. So far, he's contented himself with building a chain of check cashing and gun shops stretching from Las Vegas south and east as far as El Paso."

The helicopter banked toward a blank disc of sandy ground surrounded by low-growing creosote bushes and scattered mesquite and Palo Verde trees. The landing site was an almost invisible cattle watering hole. As the chopper settled on the ground, the water drained away and the whole "pond" surface started lowering, like the elevators on an aircraft carrier deck. One level down she saw another "ground" panel sliding into place above. She chuckled to *herself* as she realized they were now in the bowels of a Titan missile silo — sans missile.

"In ten minutes the water will be back, along with the mud and cows," her father said. "Coming by air, we leave no tracks in or out. There's a cowboy at every corner for miles around and outside the fence are extra *migra* so illegals don't get close enough to look at our 'pond' for water on their way north."

They climbed out of the cabin and she followed him into an elevator with a door like a bank vault. Everything was thick, blast proof, Cold War gold standard. He pushed several numbers on a keypad and the door slid slowly shut without a sound.

"Swiss bearings," he said. "But a wholly owned subsidiary of an American corporation."

The elevator descended with a smoothness Tina found slightly disconcerting. The lights on the panel by the door changed to show the descent between levels, but it felt more like the earth was moving up around them. She'd prefer the G-forces and acceleration of riding Black Eagle to this eerie downward slide.

The elevator stopped midway down the list of 20 floors. There was no jarring of gravity, merely a faint change in the sound and the inward air pressure as the door opened. A positive ventilation system that would blow out any contaminant, or toxic attack, she guessed. The elevator opened into an arcade with four doors, all with keypads and scanners.

"You still haven't told me who you work for."

"'We' work for. It's 'we' now. 'We' don't exist, of course, so since we're an NGO, I suppose you could say we work for the truth."

He punched in a code on the fourth door and it slid open onto a brightly lit corridor. As he walked, he filled in the gaps left by Tina's guesswork.

"Who the heck are we...well, we built an 'extra' missile silo, but with no missile. In the 1960s, Nez had followed Victor to Washington. Nez was in DC with the Udalls, but he had actually started working into the organization deeper than Mo and Stu. When Mo had first started serving in Congress he had told some of his Arizona friends that he finally learned the difference between a cactus and a caucus — a cactus had the pricks on the outside.

"When I came back from 'Nam in 1975, I took you and your mother with me when I started working on Mo's presidential campaign. He would have been great, despite his reputation as being 'too funny to be president.'

"So, we got Jimmy Carter instead. But Mo left a legacy of good legislation, including campaign finance reforms, environmental protection, and plenty to benefit Native Americans."

He knocked on the solid wall of the tunnel. "Mo and Stu knew about the Indian casinos they helped authorize, but they never knew about this silo. I guess you could say we had gone underground by then...it was better for them that they didn't know."

"Wait, let me take a shot at this," Tina said. "That way 'they could neither confirm nor deny the existence of facilities, organizations or operations. Such information — unless it had been officially acknowledged — would be classified for reasons of national security. The mere fact of the existence or non-existence of such information or their knowledge thereof would also relate directly to information concerning intelligence sources and methods.'"

"Try that in Vietnamese. You're absolutely right. Morris and Stewart were as much in the dark about this silo as we would be if the lights went out…but they never go out."

Chester stopped at a door that looked to Tina like every other door they had passed. "So, time to get serious and go to work." He scanned his ID badge, punched in his pass code and pushed the door open.

"I still have a serious question," Tina said as she followed him in. "What's the name of this organization?"

He pushed the door closed behind her, waved her to a large table covered with white binders and a laptop. "As you can tell, we have plenty of resources, but in overall numbers there aren't that many of us. Since it's a completely unofficial, non-government organization, we've stuck with the name Bobby Kennedy used when he first dreamed the dream: We're 'The Good Guys.'"

He sat down and pulled open the first binder. "Unfortunately, as I said, there aren't that many of us." He put his arm over her shoulder as she took the seat beside him. "Fortunately, we know each other."

He tapped a few keys on the laptop and a map projected onto the whiteboard along the wall. He pointed to a reddish area that covered the entire southwest and a scattered patchwork across the country.

"Mara Salvatrucha has spread from Los Angeles into a nationwide gang, but an offshoot has been organized by a group of expatriot Colombians living in the U.S. For simplicity we'll call them the 'Ricos.' The pipeline for cocaine that ran up through Guatemala and into the U.S. via Mexico has been in place for decades. What's troubling now is that the new hierarchy we're calling MSC for Mara Salvatrucha/Colombia is taking over much of the high-profit distribution on this end.

"Jackson and his Vietnamese gang have tapped into the Las Vegas area. As with the rest of the economy, the growth is where the demographic is. The tentacles include car thefts, chop shops, and check cashing and loan operations for laundering the proceeds. Which I don't have to tell you are substantial.

"It's a big interstate business, centering in Las Vegas, Phoenix, Albuquerque, and branching out from there. The American middlemen are still buying from the east and west Mexican cartels but are becoming more involved on the supply side. Now there are two ways this could come down: The first is ugly, MSC plays the two sides against each other, which has already been going on as a sort of family feud for years.

"The alternative is that MSC makes its best deal with one and leaves the other to keep trying to work its own network while we continue to chop off the snake heads on this side of the border. We're thinking we could take advantage of MSC's urge to have a clean deal by sending someone up from inside the Ricos in Mexico, get the system set up in Vegas-Phoenix-Albuquerque, then draw the net.

"Another complication is the possibility that MSC won't have a clear control of distribution in the U.S. They've been staging a low-level turf battle on the distribution side with Jackson Truong and other Vietnamese gangs specializing in high grade marijuana from Canada."

He tapped a couple more keys and the map switched to Mexico and Central America. Again, several routes ran south to north.

"Banking and money is the bait. With the competition getting violent in Guatemala, a lot of the mid-level Ricos want out of the crossfire, but they're already on the 'not welcome' list here. Over the past year, we've set up a friendly travel agency to siphon money into numbered accounts in Guatemala and Switzerland. We're ready to bring more of the Ricos up through Mexico. Now the next domino is to work the coyote network in Nogales and connect to the stateside gangs by waving the key to the piggybank under their noses."

"And that key to the piggybank will be me."

"Exactly. As far as the border crossings for the Colombians and Guatemalans, you'll be brokering that transaction, or transactions. We have no shortage of volunteers looking to get out of Central America and into the U.S. They've been doubling for us, so this is our way to pay them back. Let's call it witness protection through the back door."

Another map, this time the whole southwest border, dotted with incident markers.

"The gun traffickers are our main target. We'll make sure the right people at ICE get a hook into the drug distribution, but our main goal is to stop the flow of weapons. Mexico is right next door and we have had too many examples of what happens when too many guns are used to topple a government. The U.S. has been a culprit itself, but that's one of the reasons the Good Guys are in business. No more United Fruit setting up 'Banana Republics.'"

Tina pointed to the room, the silo around it: "So is all this paid for by the American taxpayers?"

He smiled, passed her a fat folder. "Oh, no honey. You can read all about it here in your banking homework. There have been quite a few smart, and very wealthy, business people involved at every step of the way. You can already imagine some of the names and family ties from the Camelot era.

"It's not all altruistic. Crime is bad for business, especially when the violence affects the lives of everybody around it. You see that if you talk to some of the people in these Arizona neighborhoods who have a whole different picture of border issues than the ivory tower people in Washington."

Chester tapped the cover of the folder, the flap, as usual sealed with a glob of wax. His ring, given to him long ago by grandmother Estrella, was functional as well as decorative, she realized: The maze of I'itoi. "Money has never been a problem. Getting good people, like you, has been our operational limitation. We've had to pick our battles and this border mess strikes close to home. As for the money, whenever there's a mess like Iran-Contra or the BCCI banking scandals, we seem to find a way to provide helpful solutions to clean things up.

"Usually there's an extra bank, or missile silo, in it for us. You will be facing several challenges on your road ahead, but cash won't be one of them."

"I always suspected that you and Mama did secret work for the CIA."

He chuckled. "Sorry honey, but the words 'secret' and 'CIA' don't exactly fit in the same sentence. They're big and stupid. The way we stay low and stay small and get things done is more like the mafia model. Like the way I'm bringing you in…we keep things in the family."

"How big is the family?"

"Let's just say there are a lot of good guys in the world, and I mean just that. This wouldn't work if it were a strictly American group."

****

# Chapter 16

She flew to Geneva under diplomatic cover, took a taxi to an address that turned out to be a plain brown building a couple blocks from the Rive Gauche of the Rhone River. This "left bank" location, a few blocks away from the University, suited her itinerary – a couple days of wardrobe shopping and moderately visible bank transactions before the planned flights to Colombia and Guatemala.

A dour woman concierge opened the door at the buzzer, but melted a bit when Tina gave her a friendly greeting in perfect French. Madam Chagall showed her to a small, but extremely well furnished room on the top floor that looked out over the tiled roofs of the neighborhood. Tina would be using her German with the bankers the next few days, but planned to do her shopping *a la francaise*. After a warm shower, happy to feel the full range of motion returning to her left shoulder, it was off to *Plainpalais* and the old town *"Vielle Ville"* for a quiet dinner and then a leisurely stroll through the labyrinth of cobbled streets.

This was her second visit to Geneva. The first had been a NATO assignment to aid the defection a high-ranking Albanian eager to sell nuclear secrets in the wake of the Soviet Union's unraveling. The secrets turned out to be bogus, but so was the bank account Tina had set up for him.

Banks, the world of money; the new language she had absorbed both fascinated and appalled her.

Switzerland, routing codes, passwords, a maze of names. The fish she would be netting in Mexico had already been swimming north in small batches, now idling in Mazatlan, playing golf. Millions of dollars would soon be dancing at her fingertips here in Geneva, then she would spread it around: Banco Industrial in Guatemala, Mexico's Banamex a subsidiary of Citigroup, Bogotá Internacional, then Wells Fargo and Bank of America in the U.S. just to give herself access to plenty of cash.

Tina found a little irony in the fact that first reference to the term "money laundering" itself actually appeared during the Watergate scandal. Richard Nixon's "Committee to Re-elect the President" moved illegal campaign contributions to Mexico, then brought the money back through a company in Miami. It was Britain's Guardian newspaper that coined the term, referring to the process as "laundering."

Deep Throat had been right when he had told Woodward and Bernstein to follow the money. Now Tina was going to scatter plenty of it around to establish her credibility as a crook.

The next morning she slipped into the tight black silk suit and spike heels she had picked to give her the "banker bitch" look. She rolled her hair into a sleek chignon and put on a pair of diamond studded Armani glasses she didn't need to see with. A glossy black leather purse completed the outfit.

Doors opened, bankers bowed obsequiously and she practiced being curt in Italian, German, Russian and Japanese. The IBAN numbers flew from her fingertips and dollars flowed at her command. The International Bank Account Number was the key to routing: The alphanumeric code specified country, the bank name, the particular branch and finally the destination account.

There were thousands of codes just for the bank routings, topped by the password security procedures Tina wielded with the pompous or obsequious sycophants she encountered as she moved from bank to bank.

As the dollar flow grew during the morning, Tina found herself especially fond of one particular finishing touch: Each transaction must pass a "checksum" calculation test using a position-weighted sum of the routing digits. The string of account numbers had to run through a complicated equation where the final remainder must equal 1.

The Society for Worldwide Interbank Financial Telecommunication (SWIFT) handled the registration of these codes. For this reason, Bank Identifier Codes (BICs) were often called SWIFT addresses or codes.

To validate the addresses, the four initial characters were moved to the end of the string. The letters in the string were replaced with digits, A=10 and Z=36. Then the string was added up to a single integer, run through a "mod 97-10 calculation" and if the remainder was 1 you had a valid IBAN number.

In the U.S., the similar system was supposed to take the 17 digit routing code and deliver a modulo remainder of zero, so Tina had worked out her own emergency signal: If she was compromised and being forced to make a transaction, she would keypad a string that would not be zero. Instead, the remainder digit would trigger a coded alert message deep inside the silo in Arizona.

The last step before leaving each bank was a stop at the shredder to destroy all paper transaction records, thank you very much, to the incredulous looks of the staffers.

A light lunch at one of Geneva's excellent French restaurants was followed by an afternoon of shopping. The first stop was the most important: A leather merchant had been sent an advance order. Tina opened the larger case, appreciating the fine, smooth lambskin leather, and ran her fingers over the silk lining. The compartment was invisible and according to specs would have an ingrained mesh of lead in a pattern that would fool airport security.

The second case was slightly smaller and could nest inside the larger one if necessary. Each held invisible electronic tracking and security circuits.

From the second case, Tina picked up a pair of beautiful boots. At least they were beautiful now: the lugged soles showed they were meant to handle rough miles. She had designed them herself. The deep brown leather was Vietnamese water buffalo, tough but flexible and waterproof. The front lacing allowed for several sock or lining combinations, the strap around the top guaranteed a snug fit below the calf and the gusseted zipper on the inside was invisible when closed, but could open quickly in an emergency. The final touch was an invisible sleeve inside the lining above and slightly behind the right ankle. It was for the knife. The left boot held a similar cache for "toys" — electronic devices which were usually drab looking compared to the movie versions with their switches, timers and flashing lights.

The shopping on day two was more visible. At each designer shop, she strode in carrying the bag from the previous store and bought increasingly expensive outfits. The irony was that the higher the price tags, the lighter and filmier the fabrics.

The toughest fit had been at the swimwear emporium. Tina had finally selected a classic Bardot-style bikini in polka dots. The saleswoman had assured her it was no problem to substitute the smaller size bikini bottom so as to adequately match her "excellent figure." Her only scar was on her lower back — shrapnel from her first assignment with the Marine Corps Security Force Regiment in the invasion of Panama after graduating from Annapolis. Tina figured nobody at the beach would be looking at the scar.

She'd had a cab troll with her along the row of boutiques. The seat was now stacked with bags, but Tina figured that without the wrappings, the whole pile of boodle would fit in the two new suitcases.

Was she being followed? Probably, but she was simply creating a "prequel" to the saga she was about to enact. She would go out of her way to be increasingly visible when she got to Colombia.

# Chapter 17

The smiling customs agent looked at her Colombian passport. "Welcome to Bogotá, Señorita Ochoa. Are you here for business or pleasure?"

"Business, *siempre negocios*," Tina said.

"Anything to declare?" He leafed through the colorful bouquet of frilly underwear she had purposely left on the top layer of her suitcase.

"No."

He snapped the lid of the suitcase closed.

"And what line of business are you in?" he asked, stamping the passport page and looking her square in the eye as he held it out to her.

"Finance," she said, slipping the passport into her purse and walking out past the machine gun-toting guards who lined the walkways at El Dorado International Airport.

Before she had boarded the Avianca flight in Geneva, she had made a wire transfer to an account at a small S&L in Tubac, Arizona. Anyone going to the street address would find no bank, only a sleepy street of art galleries. The bank existed only in the paper world. She was the only depositor, but her deposit of one hundred dollars — and one cent — would be duly noted.

When she reached the airport lobby, a chauffer holding the "Ochoa" card took her suitcase and shepherded her to a curbside limousine. Another uniformed man sat at the wheel. The car would not have been left alone, she knew.

She slid into the back seat, gave the driver, then her escort a thorough look as he closed the door behind them. They were both about 30, dark-skinned and sporting the short moustaches currently in vogue in Colombia.

She smiled. *"Ya'at'eeh,"* she said. Their smiles and nods told the story. She got a laugh to herself that the British MI5 had always referred to their CIA brethren as "cousins." They had nothing on the Good Guys.

The Navajo on the right pulled a familiar looking folder from the glove box. Papa must have had a single-source supplier for the durable buff envelopes. And wax seals...antiquated, but effective. It would not be difficult to duplicate the circular maze pattern of papa's ring, but she figured none of these folders were in danger of falling into the wrong hands. It was equivalent to the "single use" pads the spy boys favored for their secret messages.

Safely ensconced in her hotel room high atop a tower that looked out at the gleaming city, backed by emerald cliffs, Tina broke the seal. The Blanco family had arrived in Mazatlan, Mexico, where she would join them for the last underground leg of their trip into the U.S. There were also contact instructions and a *"bién viaje"* from papa. Once she reached Mexico she would be traveling solo.

Her biorhythms were still yo-yoing back from the week in Geneva, so she called room service for a small steak and large salad. The folder and its contents were ash by the time her meal arrived. The wax seal, it turned out, was also an excellent fire starter.

The next morning she walked the three blocks to the *Bogotá Internacional* bank office. It was not unusual for large sums to be routed through the bank, but judging from the glances she received, it was unusual for a woman to be coding the funds transfer. This transaction was a nice round one million dollars...and two cents.

Tina spent the rest of the day strolling the Avenida, glancing in shop windows, picking out a few trinkets for her meeting with the Blancos. Antonio Blanco was a loyal cog in the cocaine world. A "mid-management suck-up" was the term invented by cynics. In Antonio's case, a chance to double for the Americans in the 1990s was now paying off. He had become important enough that he feared the violence that was creeping closer to his rung of the ladder, so he wanted to punch his "get out of jail" card Uncle Sam had given him. Along for the ride were his wife Bonita, mother Luz, and four children in their teens: one girl, three boys.

So what do you get for surly teens from a cocaine cartel family? Uzis were out, so she settled on fanny packs they could cram with their own stuff. She figured some walking would probably be involved in the border crossing.

She had an early flight the next day, Copa Airlines into Tocumen International Airport in Panama City, then a connection to La Aurora Airport in Guatemala City.

A welcoming committee would attract attention at this stage, so she took a cab into Guatemala City's "Zona Viva" and checked in at the Real InterContinental.

Her sense of security was finely tuned and at full alert as she left her luggage in the luxurious suite, exited out the front door of the hotel, and made a highly visible shopping trip. "Zona Viva" could turn into "Zona Muerta" if she didn't watch her step.

The million-dollar nest egg was right where she expected it the next morning at the Banco Industrial. She transferred exactly half of it into Mexico's Banamex, then headed for the airport for the Aeronaves de Mexico flight to Mazatlan.

This time she passed through customs with a Guatemalan passport as Señorita Valentina Corazón, rode an open-air jeep into the old town, and checked into the Playa Antigua Hotel. The Blancos were out along the beach boulevard in the more modern El Cid. Tina preferred the old brick hotels that stood along the small bay, backed by the crowed *mercado*. She called and arranged a breakfast with Antonio Blanco, then settled in to rest, lulled by the sound of the waves splatting against the sea wall.

She pictured herself atop the mesa pushing sand and rocks into a pattern. That was how life worked: a push here, a turn there, look back and it's over. She prayed that the turns ahead would lead her to Ruben's murderer.

**\*\*\*\***

# Chapter 18

The wall floated in the sky, clouds above, mountains below. The corner of the wall loomed in front of Tina, the bricks solid, marked with symbols, writing in many languages. The ruddy brickwork and the chiseled messages stretched to infinity in both directions, receding into nothingness.

To the right stood a silhouette, a shadow, a ghost imprinted into the brickwork, much like the wall shadows she had seen on her trip to Nagasaki with mama Michelle.

To the left stood another shadow, a reverse shadow glowing with light. She could see through the outline of the form, through the wall, through the sky, through the dream into an awareness that she was here/not here. She let her mind float.

Above the wall another of the light silhouettes floated, arms outstretched, embracing, reaching toward the unseen horizon that was blocked by the wall.

Dream Tina pushed forward to read the inscriptions on the wall. A muttering of voices, mantras and chants echoed against her, growing louder as she neared the wall and the inscriptions came into focus. Symbols and letters burned black against the rusty background of brick: cuneiform, hieroglyphs, kanji blended with undecipherable inscriptions. She had to see, had to read, pushed forward until she could touch the rough surface with a dream hand.

Two bricks glowed at eye level. To the left she read, "Do This." To the right, "Don't Do That." She felt herself turning in her sleep, kicking against the covers to bring the wall into better focus.

Instead, the wall backed away. The harder she pushed, the further back it went. The three dream shadows had turned to watch her, their faces, one dark, two light, masks of inscrutability.

Why was the wall floating? Could she crawl under, fly over or simply push against it? The mountains far below began to glow orange. As the same orange suffused the wall, a door slowly dissolved into the brickwork, leading through into an infinite panorama.

Dream Tina looked at the three shadows in turn, rubbed the two "Do/Don't" bricks and stepped through the door...

...Into a pre-dawn glow on the *bahia*. A swishing sound below her window turned out to be the gray-bearded proprietor dousing sections of the sidewalk in front of the hotel with a bucket and then sweeping away the puddles. From the corner by the Mercado a stout woman with a limp pushed a wheeled cart, singing out *"Naranjas! Se vende naranjas!"*

Oranges indeed. Tina grabbed a pair of shorts to go with the tank top she had slept in, walked down the stairs, bought an orange from the woman and perched on the sea wall, peeling the fruit and eating it a section at a time.

The peel went into a sidewalk trash bin and Tina climbed down the steps cut into the sea wall for a quick dip in the bay. She swam a hundred meters out from the wall, still testing her left shoulder, but not finding the smallest twinge or weakness.

Flipping onto her back, she frog-kicked back to the steps. She walked slowly back to the hotel, letting her clothes drip dry in the morning air. After a shower, she took the two suitcases with her when she checked out, anticipating the unexpected when she connected with the Blancos.

She was not disappointed. She rode a pedal-cab to the El Cid. The young driver excitedly pointed out the statues, the hot disco on the point of the bay, the new hotels stretching along the sandy beach into the distance. Gaudily painted taxis honked and rolled by, stereos thumping. Her impromptu guide shrugged it off and kept talking all the way to the twin towers of El Cid. The unexpected surprise was that there were eight, not seven, in the private dining room. Antonio Blanco rose to greet her, darting a nervous glance to the stranger: a scowling younger version of Pancho Villa looming over the end of the breakfast table.

"Señorita Corazón, so nice to see you again." He had been well coached, seeing as how they had never met. "Please, let me present Carlos Cabrera. He has been sent here from Nogales by Señor de Ochenta to make final arrangements for our journey. I was telling him that we have been under your instructions to this point."

Cabrera stood, but did not offer a hand. Instead, he gave Tina a sinister head-to-toe examination. "So who the hell are you?"

She forced a cool version of a smile. "I'm the person with the money."

"So where's the money, in your suitcases?"

She tapped her temple *"Aqui, pendejo,* and in the bank."

He scowled, took a step toward her before thinking better of it.

"We're the customers," she told him coldly. "You take us to Nogales, I'll have a nice talk with Señor de Ochenta and I won't mention anything about your crappy customer service."

He crumpled his napkin and threw it onto the corner of the table. "Be out front at nine tonight," he snarled.

Tina watched him stride away. Carlos Cabrera. She would make sure not to let him get behind her.

\*\*\*\*

# Chapter 19

The ride to Nogales was a swift night passage in four black SUVs that looked strikingly like the one Tina had seen explode in the desert by Gila Bend.

Northeast of Puerto Peñasco, the Mexican police had set up a check point, but the convoy simply drove through at 80 mph without stopping

Cabrera had Tina ride with him and Blanco in the second vehicle. Tina spent the miles staring at Cabrera while Blanco dozed. Miles of warehouses and *maquiladora* workshops marked the southern edge of Nogales as the sun lightened the sky. The convoy wove through the industrial district, passed a guarded gate and climbed a well-paved road to a palatial estate surrounded by mature Cyprus trees reaching to the sky.

Señor Juan de Ochenta himself greeted them in the grand entry hall, shaking hands and smiling with a relaxed look as only a man surrounded by bodyguards could. His wavy dark hair looked real and the slightly soft face and lowered midsection put him at just a couple years over 40.

*"Bienvenidos, mis amigos.* You will stay with me while we arrange for your swift journey."

With a wave of his hand, Blanco's wife Bonita, mother Luz and the bored looking teens were escorted to another part of the house. De Ochenta turned and led the way to an oval office whose thick windows looked like they could ward off everything from machine gun fire to grenades. He waved Blanco and Tina to a couple of cushy chairs in front of his desk and went to sit in a high-back swivel chair that probably had Kevlar under the leather.

Cabrera sat off to the side, his scowl muted, but his hooded eyes wary. Tina subconsciously stretched, as if stiff from the car ride, and squeezed the ankle of her boot.

While de Ochenta and Blanco went through the casual banter regarding common acquaintances in the cocaine club from Colombia and Mexico, Tina scanned the office. The six tall windows alternated with mahogany panels. Each section of wall held a painting, but she was surprised to see that they were all painted on black velvet and framed with elaborate gilt woodwork.

It had been years since she had seen a velvet painting, and even then, never such as these. The subjects were the usual: Elvis, Jesus looking to heaven, a swirling matador and a mostly nude Aztec beauty. But the brushwork was not the casual daubing of factory art. These were masterpieces, the brushwork bright but deft, giving the subjects a luminescence that seemed to glow from within.

Señor de Ochenta had spotted her scrutiny. "You like my collection, sí? These are, of course, the originals. Many copies were made over the years, but none to compare with the masters."

"They are excellent, señor. Did you collect them?"

His smile dimmed a fraction. "No, señorita. They were commissioned by my late father before his untimely death."

From 37 rounds of automatic weapons fire on Christmas Eve, two years ago, Tina recalled from the files.

"My condolences, señor. I understand Señor Blanco is eager to complete his journey, so if you wouldn't mind, I would like to rest a bit before the bank opens. Then we can finalize the financial transaction."

His smile brightened.

Tina was shown to a room that faced an interior courtyard to rest and freshen up before her excursion to the bank. Her suitcases sat on the bed. A quick check showed that they had been opened, and searched, but not compromised. All her equipment was hiding in plain sight. The most important tools were the series of alpha-numeric codes stashed between her ears.

In addition to flipping the room's hotel style door latch, she propped a straight-back chair against the door handle, a low-tech but effective deterrent. A few stretches and a quick kata led up to a cat nap.

A couple hours later, she was escorted to the bank by a twenty-something muscle boy named José Martinez. He was wary, like Carlos Cabrera, but not as sinister. He wore dark glasses but the stern look he affected hadn't yet had a chance to etch itself deep into his cheeks.

When he took her to the car, a black Mercedes this time, he didn't protest when she sat in the front seat. She held her black purse on her lap, but it was mostly for show. Aside from the Guatemalan passport and a pair of dark glasses, the purse was empty.

"Where are you from, José?" she began a casual attempt to decipher whether he was as much of a threat as Carlos.

"Why do you want to know?" he countered. At the bottom of the hill, he stopped and rolled down the window so the guard could look inside the Mercedes.

As the gate swung open, Tina tried the friendly approach: "Look, as long as we're going to be working together, I think it would be good to get to know each other."

He smirked. "We're not working together. You're paying us to do a job."

"I was only hoping to find a warmer reception from someone than I got from Carlos."

José wove through the warehouse district before turning onto the highway that led to the "Ciudad Viejo," the old part of Nogales scattered along the Rio Santa Cruz. The stacks of colorful adobe houses perched on the cliffs stopped abruptly where they butted up against the dull brown border wall.

"Let me tell you something about Carlos. Don't trust him. It's not that he hates you. He hates everybody. Señor de Ochenta keeps Carlos around as his personal attack dog. How's that for friendly advice?"

"Can I trust you?" Tina tried out her sincerest phony smile.

"Hell no," he said, turning onto a side road to avoid the tail end of the traffic line for the border crossing. "And I won't trust you."

"Great," she said. "There's something we can agree on."

The Nogales branch of Banamex was a squat cube covered in pale green tile. A safe little subsidiary of Citigroup, its computer system responded instantly to Tina's coding.

She got part of the transaction in cash: $200,000 in crisp new American Benjamins fit neatly into her empty purse.

The rest, a cool million, slipped into Antonio Blanco's "assembly" account she had set up for him in Turkey, routed through Switzerland as a cutout, then to another new account right here in Banamex. Then it was a simple internal transfer from Blanco's account into Juan de Ochenta's. She even had a nice VISA card printed up in de Ochenta's name, no photo thank you very much, for the *patrón* to use in case he ever found himself without bodyguards, assassins, servants and hangers-on.

In less than an hour Tina was back on the sidewalk heading for the Mercedes, the bank manager Señor Rosales insisting on escorting her as she carried the sleek black purse stuffed with cash.

José saw her coming and clicked the door latches open. This time, Tina sat in the back.

They circled Calle Obregón, past the tethered photo donkeys, gringos searching for the "best price" on tequila and stooped retirees seeking to refill their prescriptions. At one traffic-choked intersection, the car came to a complete stop in front of an alley packed with *"los Indios"* hawking woven baskets, toys and painted animal figurines.

"Wait for me at the corner," Tina shouted as she jumped out of the car and disappeared into the alley. A few minutes later, she found the Mercedes blocking the next alley, with José steaming at the wheel and ignoring the honking drivers backed up behind him.

'Drive on, *caballero*," she said as she jumped into the back seat. "Look at this great money bag I bought." She waved the striped straw tote across the seatback next to him.

"Don't ever do that again," he snarled. "You're likely to get us both killed."

"I didn't know I was in custody," Tina said with exaggerated lightness. "I left that big purse full of cash on the seat, so where was I going to go? The deal is, I stay with the Blancos until they get to Phoenix. Besides, this is just the first batch of cash. I have to do a couple more transfers in the next few days."

They rolled sporadically through the densest part of the tourist section now. Sidewalk hawkers called to her through the window of the Mercedes: "Shop here, señorita, best prices."

Americans in shorts and tank tops filled the sidewalk. On every block there was one, but only one, beggar, usually a Oaxacan Indian mother with a small urchin brandishing a box of Chiclets. Tina wondered if they worked shifts.

José turned the corner in front of the cathedral. Street vendors packed the sidewalk in front of the church steps.

"How about I buy us some tamales?" Tina offered.

No response.

She reached into the bag for her secret weapon, a yellow wooden popgun, the cork already loaded. She brandished it at him in the mirror: "You tough guys don't scare me!"

He stared back in the reflection for a couple seconds, finally lost the battle not to smile. He held out his hand: "You'd better hand that over before it goes off."

The rest of the trip was silent but relaxed. As they climbed the ridge to the fortress, Tina saw a line of afternoon thunderheads on the horizon. Rain. The border crossing plan for the Blanco family called for a July monsoon to clear the way through the tunnels under the Nogales border.

Rain in the desert, though, was unpredictable. There could be traces, hints, threats of rain, but no droplets. Just as suddenly, a deluge in another place could send a flash flood down the washes and rivers to wash away everything under a wall of water.

Tina resolved to keep her eyes open for those unseen deluges. One such unexpected disaster had swept Ruben away.

# Chapter 20

And so that monsoon crossing through the tunnel had ended in disaster despite her wariness. She woke up with a blood pressure cuff on her arm this time. The plastic handcuffs were gone. The uniformed woman had a badge with an eagle on top of it and a round patch on her left sleeve. Border Patrol. Tina remembered the flooded tunnel, the redhead knocking her in the skull, the Blanco family hijacked from the Border Patrol bus.

Most of all, she remembered her cover: *"Donde estamos?"* She turned, saw a pair of men in uniforms, one holding a clipboard. *"Donde estan los otros?"*

The woman squeezed the bulb, released the valve and watched Tina's pulse on the dial. She wrote something on a form, took off the cuff and walked over to the men. Overhead, the halogen lights of the warehouse made a slight buzzing, punctuated by the occasional sizzle of a moth immolating itself.

"Her blood pressure is fine, but she looks like she had a concussion."

"We got a hit on her ID," said clipboard man. "We're supposed to personally escort her to processing at Florence." He held up Tina's passport, matching it to the form on the clipboard. "It looks like our little Señorita Corazón gets a solo ride in the van."

The woman agent gave them a quizzical look: "She's on the watch list? She doesn't look dangerous."

"Could be a witness or something. It just says expedited processing."

The woman signed the clipboard he handed her and the two men helped Tina to her feet and steered her to the back seat of a passenger van. Another set of handcuffs, the expensive stainless steel type this time.

When the van pulled out from the halogen glare of the warehouse, Tina realized it was still the middle of the night. She had the bench seat to herself and surrendered to the blackness again.

The red brick dream wall appeared again, floating in the darkness. This time there was no door. She groped her way along the rough surface. Each inscribed brick murmured a directive at her as her fingertips sought a gap, a handhold, a clue.

Stymied, she turned away from the wall. A blank horizon stretched before her. The three dream figures were gone. She was alone.

A sunlit reflection woke her. She pushed herself up to look out the window and recognized the cotton fields by Eloy. Dizziness and a dull ache forced her head back down on the seat. The rolling motion of the van made her queasy.

"Hey, honey, do you speak English?" the driver hollered back at her. She ignored him, closed her eyes again and feigned sleep, although her continuing dizziness was real.

"She's too cute to be a terrorist," the driver said.

"Shut up and drive," said his companion. "For all you know, she could be a regular Mata Hari from FARC or the PLO. You notice she doesn't look like your garden variety Mexican or Guatemalan. Her passport says Quetzaltenango, but she has a little bit of Arab look to her if you ask me."

"Well, with a body like that, she could sure Mata Hari me."

Blackness again. No more wall this time, but a succession of van doors slamming, rolling on some kind of gurney, people talking, but mostly the blackness. When consciousness came back, it had to battle dizziness to see who was boss.

Another hospital room, another guard, this time in a U.S. Marshals uniform. The only thing that set him apart from the previous batch was "the look."

"*Ya'at'eeh*," she called to him.

He responded in kind and went out the door. Tina relaxed; she was back with the good guys.

More sleep, this time dreams of exploding trucks and flooded *tunnels*. Ruben was calling to her from the depths of one of the tunnels: "*Cuidado, Tausongatina*. Be careful."

The next time she woke up the room was dark, but the dizziness had subsided. The headache was an echo of its former throb. She climbed from her bed and tiptoed to the door. Opening it a crack, she spotted her bodyguard again.

"Don't worry, I'm not going to make a break for it," she told him. "Do you think you could rustle up a hamburger from room service or call out for a pizza?"

"I'll see what I can do."

Tina climbed back into bed. We see what we can do, she mused. What could she do now? She rewound her memory tapes of the chain of events: Ruben murdered. The Blanco family hijacked but most likely delivered to a destination of their own choosing after she had been cut out of the deal.

She thought she had a handle on the list of primary bad guys: The redhead bastard led the field on the American side. He was in a dead heat with the yet unseen Jackson Truong.

In Nogales, Carlos Cabrera was the lead suspect in Ruben's murder. Juan de Ochenta was the center of the pustule, but probably didn't pull the trigger.

In addition to the supporting cast of thugs and guards, that left José Martinez. Tina hadn't made up her mind about him yet. He seemed more of a chauffer than an apprentice bad guy. She bet that without those dark glasses he was just a poseur.

Uniformed hamburger delivery came through the door. A side of potato salad also rode the tray.

Between bites, Tina quizzed her doorkeeper: "What's your name, soldier?"

"Chuy Begay."

"Another one of the Begay Brigade, eh?" she kidded him "You guys must have your own recruiting network." Begay or Begaye was about as common a name on the reservation as Smith or Jones outside.

He smiled. "Your father will be here in the morning."

She finished the last bite of the burger and handed him the tray. "Thanks, cuz."

Her next sleep was more restful: No explosions, no tunnels, no floating walls. This time, she was on the mesa looking at the maze in the sand. She realized the she had made this maze and that many other mazes were made by other hands.

She knelt over the twists and turns and began erasing the pattern in the sand. If she could not find a way through the maze, she would make one. With both hands she scooped a wide path right through the center of the coils: a Middle Way. Oh, Buddha, you Navajo trickster.

\*\*\*\*

# Chapter 21

She awoke at dawn and looked around her room. Her boots were here, but no other clothing.

Breakfast was not the feast the midnight hamburger was: juice, cottage cheese, a slab of egg-like substance. Papa Chester arrived as Chuy Begay took away the remains.

He pulled a chair up to her bedside.

"You got hit in the head pretty hard, daughter. The doctors say the second concussion was worse than the first."

He took her hand. "They're concerned that another concussion could cause permanent damage. I'm taking you off the case."

Like hell, she thought, yanking her hand from his grasp.

"No way! I'm not giving up. I owe it to Ruben, and now I've got a personal score to settle with these bastards."

He nodded, but looked unconvinced.

"Listen, Papa. I've seen the greed in these guys. I get back, raise a stink, they see I'm in it for keeps and have a grudge to settle. You don't think they suspect I'm one of the good guys, do you?"

"No. The Blanco family made it to Phoenix as per the plan, but they swear they had nothing to do with you getting booted."

"My point exactly. De Ochenta probably saw all the cash I routed into his account, figured he'd set me up for a fall with *la migra,* and keep the change. He's probably guessed after seeing this wimp Blanco that he's in no danger from little fish from Colombia. With his muscle men around him, he probably is right."

He considered that for a bit. "I'm not so sure you can count on him being predictable. What if you go back and they decide to simply kill you?"

"C'mon, Papa. I've seen de Ochenta up close. He's second or third generation and softer than the ruthless pricks who sired him."

His eyebrows raised a notch in reaction to her word choice, but she forged ahead.

"They probably figure I'm stuck in the immigration zoo here while they're sitting on their two million bucks. We do an end run: Get me deported to Guatemala. I access the Nogales bank remotely and clean out de Ochenta's account. Since I put the cash there, I know how to siphon it off or track wherever he tried to hide it. I make sure there's a zero balance."

He nodded. "Then they'll really want to kill you."

"Except for one thing." She tapped her forehead. "The numbers are in here."

His frown gave him the "Viejo" look again.

"What about torture?"

"Forget it, Papa. I'm a Marine. I can hold out long enough that they would believe me if I tell them to take me to the bank, I give up. Then I send the SOS code through IBAN. Better yet, I transfer the funds to a U.S. site with instructions to release only on my safe arrival. That's not likely to happen, though." A trace of a smile as an idea began hatching.

"It sounds like you have another option in mind."

"Correct. I clean out the account, but go back and accuse somebody of setting me up. I tell de Ochenta that I still have more Colombians ready to migrate, but that he has to do it my way. That shows my loyalty to the Colombians and makes him trust me. Plus, he'll be greedy to get his cash back, including more money on top of that. There's only one problem."

"Only one?"

"Well, the first one that comes to mind is that I'm going to need a big fish to make the second deal with de Ochenta believable. Can you come up with one?"

"Don't worry, we have a bottomless supply of bad guys ready to hide from their pasts."

"One last thing — get me out of here. I need to do some research at the silo."

****

# Chapter 22

On the way down to the situation room, Chester stopped at a door marked storage. He gave Tina a wink, punched in the code, pushed open the door and stepped back to let her look.

Gleaming under the lights sat Black Eagle. The dents, scrapes and bullet holes were gone. Neatly painted on the tank were two new items: silhouettes of a semi and an SUV with red "Xs" through them. Her leathers and a new helmet hung on a peg near the bike.

"I decided you might be able to squeeze in a day of R&R before you fly back to Guatemala."

She gave him a hug.

"Thanks, Papa, but I have another "R" in mind. There's an area I want to recon, and Black Eagle will be the perfect way to scout at ground level." She tapped the panniers: "The usual assortment of toys?"

He nodded and gave her directions to an exit tunnel that she could use, bypassing the helicopter lift.

When they got to the computer room, she wanted to look through the paper files from Fort Benning to take a close look at the Grupo Zetas, the younger Zetas of a few years ago. Maybe she could recognize some more faces and connect them with her recent memory in Nogales.

She sorted through the records, the obstacle course times and weaponry proficiency tests, looking at each name, coming up with nothing. Then a graduation day photo caught her eye. The group was standing at attention, shiny new paratrooper "jump" wings gleaming on starched uniforms. On the end with the American instructors stood the red-headed bastard, this time in an Army uniform.

She cranked up the resolution and zoomed in closer. Even in black and white, she was sure the photo was him.

She started scrolling face by face.

On the other end was an instructor who looked like Ruben…she hadn't known he had been assigned as an instructor at Fort Benning. This guy was tall like Ruben, but much more slender, had a moustache and shaved head. They all had the same haircut, but the moustache rate was about 60 percent.

"Papa, look." She pointed to the photo. "Was Ruben an instructor at Benning?"

"Not to my knowledge." He dialed up the resolution on the screen another notch, leaned closer to examine the photo.

"He's not an instructor," he said, pointing to the insignia on Ruben's shoulder. "This was taken after he had already made the transition under cover in Mexico."

"Jesus. So he was a Zeta." She studied the details again. Ruben must have dropped fifty pounds to lose his Samoan bulk. The moustache tipped the balance to make him look 100 percent Mexican.

The realization of how thoroughly her cousin had worked his way into the Mexican underground impressed Tina, but also left a chill when she considered the ruthless self-cleansing and aggressive recruitment the vicious organization practiced.

"Did any Zetas stay on the *Federales'* side?"

"A few did, yes, but most of those were later killed. As you can imagine, that has also put a damper on recruiting efforts by the police and military."

"It doesn't really matter. He's dead," Tina said grimly. She placed a finger on the scowling face of the red-headed American. "What can we get on this guy?"

"Let me check." He noted the redhead's position in the photo and went to another terminal.

Tina zoomed back out and looked again at the orderly rows, the firm posture. Something wasn't quite right. The setup was the same as every other jump school photo she had ever seen: the row in front kneeling, short guys in the middle, tall guys in back, heads offset so "if you can see the camera, the camera can see you."

One soldier was out of position, either by accident or deliberately breaking that rule. She zoomed in, got just the slice of face, an ear, part of the moustache, half an eyebrow and just the edge of the scowl: Carlos Cabrera.

Of course, that name was not on the books. Neither would Ruben's name surface in any of the records.

Tina went back to the stack of paper files. Sorting through the black and white firing range and obstacle course action shots, she found two more photos that looked like Carlos. She grabbed a magnifying glass and studied the pictures grain by grain. She was certain it was him.

"I got a hit on your redhead," her father called out.

She went over and sat at the seat next to his terminal.

"Unfortunately, the news is bad. He enlisted under the name Sean Keating, but that turned out to be an alias. After he turned up AWOL, the trace back found that he was in the country illegally. Worse, he was undercover for the IRA."

He turned and gave her a quizzical look: "What made you single him out?"

"That's the bastard who waved Vegetable Man through the customs station at Naco."

She let that sink in for just a second. "He's also the guy who brained me in Nogales and sidetracked Arturo Blanco and his family."

"Damn," he said, about the roughest language she ever heard him use. "You think he could be Ruben's killer?"

"A 50-50 chance. Check this out."

She showed him the grainy photos of Carlos Cabrera and told him about the rough welcome he dished out. "My theory is that Juan de Ochenta is sitting in the chair, but that Carlos is running the show."

They sorted through the photos one last time. Tina paused to stare at a shot of Ruben climbing the rope on the O-course. It amazed her that a man that big could be so strong. She slipped the photo back in the stack and weighed the grudge she was now carrying against Carlos Cabrera and this Sean Keating. The grudge would most likely get heavier, but she would carry it. She was ready to do what needed to be done.

Chester's computer beeped an incoming alert. He went over to it and glanced through the file.

"Got another hit on your Keating. The photos matched the Border Patrol files for Naco and Nogales at the times of your incidents. This time he's going by Sean MacDonald."

"And he's disappeared."

"From there, yes," he said. "But not completely. Our tracking on Jackson Truong reports that he was seen last week with a red-headed man matching Sean Keating/MacDonald's description."

He spun his chair to face her. "They were at the Paris Air Show."

**\*\*\*\***

148

# Chapter 23

Black Eagle fired up on the first crank. While the motorcycle warmed up, Tina slipped into her leathers.

She zipped the pants first: Two long zippers on the lower legs and one in the front. The Vanson pants were always the best indicator of whether she was winning the battle of the thighs.

No tugging required and she could still breathe when she stood up. Excellent. The jacket slipped on and zipped equally well. She buckled the helmet, flipped the visor up and goosed the throttle.

Tina walked the bike down the hallway toward the exit tunnel. Papa Chester stuck his head out of the Ops room and gave her a thumbs-up.

The blast door that accessed the tunnel opened slowly and silently when she punched in her code. A string of lights down the center of the ceiling looked like upside-down landing lights and she felt herself resisting the urge to do a "Tron" maneuver and zoom into the distance.

She did recall that the tunnel was supposed to be about a mile long, so she straddled Black Eagle and idled down the center, the lights blinking by overhead and reminding her of the reflections in the astronauts' helmets in "2001."

*Enough with the science fiction movies*. She had taken an elective class in film history during graduate school at Cal Tech. Tonight was more like Jane Bond again. Too late to turn back at this stage of the maze.

The exit door required another set of passwords and opened into an empty barn, which, in turn, demanded the right authorizations and sequences.

When she could finally click Black Eagle into gear and twist the throttle, Tina found herself weaving through a dry pasture that abutted a dirt road. A low-tech wire fence with a livestock gate opened onto the dirt road. She turned west and connected to the frontage road along Interstate 10 north of Tubac. The granite dome of Elephant Head watched from her right.

She was heading for the Tohono O'odham Reservation and Baboquivari Peak in particular, so she blasted north on I-10 for a handful of miles and turned west at Arivaca Junction. It was just about midnight, and a smattering of bar patrons clustered outside the huge stucco cow skull façade of the Arivaca Tavern. Tina honked her horn and rode west with the night.

A half hour later, she idled down and rolled slowly through town as Arivaca slumbered, but a faint trace of marijuana aroma floated in the air.

A winding uphill slalom crossed the Sierrita Mountains, and the left-right weight shifts perked her up. On the downhill side, she found herself sliding across the saddle, downshifting into the turns and clipping the apexes. She even touched a knee on one off-camber decreasing-radius bend.

That woke her up and she eased off on the throttle. No sense killing herself on the highway when there was no shortage of thugs who might want to.

She rolled down into the cool night air of the Buenos Aires Wildlife Refuge and turned north on Arizona Route 286. Ahead in the darkness to her left rose Baboquivari, and beyond that Kitt Peak with its astronomers toiling the night away to understand the universe.

Tina had a more down to earth goal. She eased up still more on the gas and shifted into third gear as she kept an eye open for the cattle guard that marked her turn.

It was all dirt from here. The Tohono O'odham Reservation was the third largest in the country after the Navajo and Utes. That was only counting the portion in the United States. A third of the tribe lived across the border in Mexico and the people did not make a distinction about nationality. North or south of the border, they were all Tohono O'odham.

This wreaked havoc on border enforcement, too, as birth certificates and identification were somewhat sketchy with a people who had grown accustomed to walking through the gate in the barbed wire border fence any time there was a family event on the other side.

In the darkness, Tina picked her way along increasingly rugged uphill trails until she reached the spine of the ridge that linked north to Baboquivari and south into Mexico. To the west lay hundreds of miles of desert stretching to Yuma, the sludgy remnants of the Colorado River and then California.

To call it trackless desert would be a misnomer. Many illegal immigrants died every year trying to follow the trails that scattered across the landscape. A few years earlier, Tina herself had put her tracking skills to use out here when she had first been assigned to the Border patrol. Grandfather Nez had taught her how to look carefully for signs and read into them the person who left them.

Tina had worked with new agents from the Tohono O'odham and other tribes recruited as trackers for the Border Patrol two years ago. A dozen hand-picked agents became the "Shadow Wolves," combining native traditions and respect for the land with the vital goal of drug interdiction.

The millions of acres of sand gave subtle clues: Most prized were the deeper footprints left by drug smugglers carrying heavy backpacks. In the past couple years, literally tons of marijuana had been intercepted after the Shadow Wolves followed minute trails of crumpled grasses, broken twigs, dusty footprints or wisps of burlap snagged on thorny branches.

Tonight, Tina was working on a theory that involved higher tech devices. A lone saguaro stood like a sentinel in a crag atop the ridge. She parked Black Eagle next to it, took off her helmet, grabbed her binoculars and sat on the best rock she could find. There were several hours of darkness left in this night.

As her eyes adjusted, she could see an occasional flash of headlights in the distance toward Sells. Probably Border Patrol agents getting off work. Border enforcement had brought new residents to the tiny town and more manufactured housing sprang up by the week.

The nocturnal cat-and-mouse of the coyotes and *la migra* would be done in the dark. Tina's focus, however, was on the sky. Both eyes and ears were alert. The silence was punctuated only by her deep inhalation and exhalation as she scanned the stars, waiting for movement. At last she heard the drone. She trained the binoculars ahead of the sound to compensate for the altitude and finally saw it: without lights, it showed up more as a shadow moving in front of the stars.

The pilotless plane was basically a huge gas tank with wings that patrolled at high altitude for days without refueling. Controlled out of Fort Huachuca, it had both regular and infrared cameras in its array of electronics. Combined with old fashion helium balloons that were raised and lowered on tethers, and newer radar dishes, these eyes in the skies were all that stood in the way of a helicopter shuttle that could ferry drugs, people or weapons with impunity.

Tina had been giving a lot of thought to the abandoned hangar where Vegetable Man had met his explosive finale. From where she sat, it was only about a 100-mile flight to a rendezvous point like that along the Interstate 8 corridor to San Diego.

A walk of only five or ten miles north from Mexico would put passengers, or cargo, right here in the middle of no place for a pickup. A connecting flight on Nocturnal Airlines could easily reach as far as Phoenix or Las Vegas. A low flying chopper could bypass the deadly game of chase played by the trucks of the smugglers and the Border Patrol.

Night sounds returned: A few fluttering bats, a chorus of hoots from two great horned owls north and south of her, a distant yodel from a pack of excited coyotes. Finally, she heard the drone coming back the other direction, tracing a grid above the vast desert. She checked her watch: 37 minutes. With the right chopper, synchronized timing, and sophisticated ECM, ie. purloined electronic countermeasures, it wouldn't be too hard to hug the deck and fly under the watchful eye of Big Brother.

As the drone disappeared to the west, Tina could have sworn she heard the thumping of helicopter blades echoing along the valley floor below. It was too dark to tell.

****

# Chapter 24

Contours emerged into light. Distant clouds bloomed purple, glowed pink, then neon white as the sun's rays shot through them. Tina stood, stretched and welcomed the day once more with her litany of thanks. From her perch atop the ridge, she turned and looked west, watching the subtle shadows cling to the low areas that flowed primarily north.

The skein of trails would follow the lowlands. Wildlife, Conquistadors, cattle and smugglers had worn their marks over the centuries. These paths of least resistance also afforded cover from prying eyes and patches of shade from the blazing sun.

Tina planned a spider web of her own to put some twists into the maze. Subtle turns that couldn't be seen until they were in the rear view mirror.

From the right pannier, she took out one of the largest of her "toys." The main transponder would listen for signals across the huge flatland below. The repeater circuitry would then beam to an anonymous dish nestled among the array at the Whipple Observatory atop Mount Hopkins. She wedged it into a crack in the pink granite, the face pointing west, then locked it in place with a climbing chock.

The uplink signals would be monitored around the clock at the silo, but Tina would be alone out here when she sprung her trap. The saguaro stretched its arms as if enjoying a morning yawn. It curved upward in the classic two-arm configuration and she noticed that the shadow of one arm pointed across the valley to her next destination.

The high point was 50 miles away to the southwest. Black Eagle made smooth work of the rugged ground, churning across sand, rocks and slithering between bushes as Tina combined dead reckoning with the GPS data on her screen.

Abandoned water jugs, clothing and jackets littering the ground spoke to the human traffic. The worst was underwear occasionally strewn into the trees. The illegals hardy enough to trek this far were often prey to bandits who robbed them at gunpoint and made them strip.

Every ten miles, she would attach a mini disc to a branch or other hiding place. These were newer, smaller versions of the transponders she had scattered around Kuwait City under the noses of Saddam Hussein's garrisons.

She found a good vantage point for the southwest corner transponder and took a short water break before heading north toward Sells. This area was one of the most heavily patrolled and she kept a wary eye out for the green Border Patrol trucks. The radio scanner also kept her aware of the early morning deployment. She knew that Black Eagle could outrun any of the enforcement vehicles, but the last thing in the world she wanted was to attract attention, even from friendlies.

Ruben's murder had proven that trust was in short supply.

The northward loops in her pattern often paralleled the low washes that cut through the desert crust. As she idled along the bank of one of these sandy bottoms, Tina startled a band of javelinas that had dug themselves a wallow in the shade of a mesquite tree. The nocturnal critters had settled in the moist wash bottom to nap away the day. At night they would forage for desert morsels, one of their favorite foods being the ping pong paddle-shaped prickly pear cactus leaves.

She cut the engine and watched the little hairy gray heads stare back at her. It looked to be two families: four adults about the size of a short-legged German shepherd, and five or six "reds" — the babies giving her a squinty look. A dozen black eyes stared at her over the piglike snouts. Despite the flared nostrils and boar-shaped heads, they were actually "banded peccaries" and no relation to the pig family at all.

By the time she kick-started Black Eagle, they had been convinced she was no threat. They squinted at her with their little black eyes as she rode away.

Little by little, mile by mile and disc by disc, Tina wove her web. All the while, the read the ground for tracks. The history of human and animal traffic was written in the soft sand, hard-packed caliche, broken vegetation and displaced rocks. Wildlife sign was abundant, especially the distinctive cross-shaped tracks left by road runners. Instead of a forked print like other birds, the road runner print was literally an "x" shape that took close examination to discern the direction of the bird's travel.

Of more interest to Tina were the human prints, most showing battered athletic shoes or round-heeled cowboy boots.

East of the Tohono O'odham village of San Miguel, a set of footprints with Vibram soles caught her eye. Those particular prints were left by rugged hiking boots and the depth of the pattern indicated the wearer was carrying a heavy load. She idled through the desert in Black Eagle's lowest off-road gear, following the trail.

It wasn't difficult, the sharp-edged soles left a trace as easy to read as a person with waffle irons on their feet. The trail led northwest. After a bit more than a mile, a similar set of prints crossed the first. Tina got off her bike and traced an outward spiral, looking for clues. She found four sets all together, all heavily loaded.

Back on the bike, she clicked into second gear. The trail was so obvious now that she had not trouble rolling after it. The tracks led to a low, open area. Tina parked and advanced on foot, noticing the sand blown outward from the center of the clearing. The two parallel imprints left by the helicopter's landing gear confirmed her suspicions.

The clearing turned out to be the remnant of a dry pond. Years of use by cattle showed in the scattered piles of decayed manure. In the rainy season there might be enough moisture to turn the clearing into a short-lived watering hole with maybe a couple inches of water.

Tina gave the horizon a 360-degree scan and figured the wallow was also low enough to escape the line-of-sight radar and visual surveillance that was already stretched thin in this area.

The cargo brought by the Vibram-shod mules had to be valuable, more so than marijuana bales, which would have been picked up by truck. Cocaine, maybe. Or, worse, contraband avionics or biological toxins to use in weapons.

Regardless, the trails had led to at least one landing zone. She backed Black Eagle away from the clearing and used a twiggy palo verde branch to brush away its tracks. She put an extra concentration of discs in a wide circle around the L.Z., toggled the location on her GPS log and went back to her criss-cross pattern.

By late afternoon she was ready to set the last of the primary uplink transponders. She had worked her way in a loop that ended on a ridge just south of Baboquivari Peak. The monolith spiked into the sky and she wondered if I'itoi was watching her from his cave above.

Legend or not, his help would be welcome in bringing her intricate plan to a successful end. She parked Black Eagle against a rocky outcropping and climbed for a few minutes. She activated the last transponder and anchored it into a fissure on a rock that faced southeast.

Looking back across the vast flats, she could see for at least a hundred miles. She scanned the southern horizon towards Mexico and imagined tourists sitting on the beach at Puerto Peñasco sipping margaritas and nibbling shrimp cocktails.

No touristing for her; there was work to continue.

Darkness was complete by the time she rolled back to the barn, keyed her entry and idled through the tunnel into the silo. She parked Black Eagle and peeled off her leathers. As she shut the door on the motorcycle, she hoped she would be back soon for another ride, but there were no guarantees.

When she got to her quarters, she called Papa Chester on the intercom and arranged to meet him in the mess hall in half an hour.

She noticed the regulation INS prisoner togs stacked neatly on her bed, but took her shower, sifted through the clothes papa had brought for her from Scottsdale and slipped into jeans and an Annapolis sweatshirt.

Over a salad and mashed potatoes, she described the deployment of her toys and her theory about the helicopter shuttle and the weapons-grade contraband.

"I think you're right," Papa told her. "My estimate is that Ruben was getting close to the details. That's why he decided to tag the truck that had the helicopter mounting brackets."

"Which makes Carlos Cabrera the main murder suspect."

"Not necessarily. We don't know where Sean the redhead went after he waved the truck through at Naco."

Tina scoured her memory, searching for any other anomaly that could provide a lead, came up blank.

"What about Sean and Truong?" she asked her father. "What's the deal with them in Paris?"

"My guess is that the show is not just about helicopters and planes. Shadowy arms merchants by the score track these shows like camp followers. In addition to the high end stuff, tons of disposable munitions trade hands."

"Unfortunately, it's a renewable resource," Tina said. She pictured the chaos around the world and was saddened to think that the supposedly "civilized" nations such as the U.S. provided much of the weaponry used in the carnage. Also, Europe was awash in the last decade from arms left over in the wake of the Soviet Union's disintegration. Anything from electronics to shoulder-fired missiles was available on the black market.

Her father slid a slim folder across the table to her. "One new item: One of the Mexican Air Force Eurocopters has gone missing. There was a skirmish at one of the regional police stations, and during the attack the *federales* moved in. When the dust cleared, it turned out the helicopter had simply flown away."

"Another inside job?"

"Unfortunately, the Zetas have a very persuasive campaign: *'Oro o plombo;'* 'Gold or lead.' It's making it tough on recruitment for both the police and military. You either take the bribes or end up dead."

"We've got to do some bribing of our own," Tina said. "Let's go down to the Ops room and see if we can get this plan to hatch."

When she got to the keyboard, Tina punched up the map of Arizona. Then she overlaid the locations of all the federal and military radar installations and their appropriate coverage radii.

She showed papa where the thinnest coverages were: coincidental to the open spaces that stretched west all the way to Yuma. She also keyed in the low-lying landing zone she had stumbled across. "There could be a dozen of these right under our noses."

She backed the screen out to a resolution of about fifty miles.

"Here's where the drone was patrolling last night," she took a ballpoint pen and waved it back and forth like a windshield wiper. When the pen reached the far end of the range and turned around, she picked up a paper clip to mark the helicopter's position. "The bad guys can zig-zag up from the south, stay low and skirt the coverages. The feds are talking about installing 'increased electronic surveillance,' but for now it's a game of blind man's bluff."

She put the pen and paper clip down and turned to face her father. "Until that happens, we're the blind men. Depending on what kind of communications Truong has set up, he can slip right past us when he's calling the shots."

She zoomed the map out still more to show the entire Tohono O'odham Reservation.

"This whole Baboquivari basin would be the perfect place to spring a trap," she turned and gave him a big smile, " — which I have taken the liberty to set. What I would like from you is the right bait."

"More money?"

"Thanks, but no. There's already plenty for me to spread around, plus what I'll get when I make my 'withdrawal' from Juan de Ochenta's account. I need more big fish, a couple names they'll be certain to know."

He frowned, picked up the pen and tapped the table. "That might take a little more time."

"I can buy us some time. I go back, say they don't realize who they're dealing with, but that if they play nice I'll bring in some more business, bigger business. Otherwise that empty bank account is just the start.

"Obviously they're not going to trust me, but I'm just as obviously keeping them under a microscope. For starters, I do a crossing that's entirely scripted: I pick the team, I call the shots, I pick the route."

She tapped the map on the screen. Chester smiled, obviously getting the picture of how she was going to set the trap.

"Everybody does it my way, plenty of money gets spread around and they learn that even in criminal capitalism, the customer is always right."

She rattled the keyboard, flipping through the helicopter spec sheets on the Eurocopter, Antonov and Bell choppers. That was just for starters. The Paris Air Show listing for avionics and electronics companies would take days to read through. Tina frowned and began to wonder if there were any industries on the planet that could compare to war and drugs. Oil, maybe.

She couldn't change the world, but she could try to fix one situation in one place. She would do what she could.

Papa stood and put his hand on her shoulder. "You worried it won't work?"

"All we can do is try." She patted his hand. "For the finale, we bring in one big Colombian. By then I will have gotten my foot in the door, maybe even crossed swords with Truong or the redhead myself. I tell them Mister Big only wants to deal with Truong, say he wants a taxi ride in the helicopter. Maybe he's old or got shot up recently and isn't real mobile.

"Somehow we've got to get to Truong and the redhead. They're the key to unlocking the weapons pipeline. While I'm doing that, it should become clearer to us what the setup was that caught Ruben out. There's no way he wouldn't have left himself a cutout. The only thing I can think of is that he got caught in some kind of internal sting.

"The best way to counter that is to find out their system, then make them think they're smarter than they actually are. I'm going to be the poison pill — greenback flavor."

\*\*\*\*

# Chapter 25

The flight back to Guatemala in casual prison attire was less than comfortable. A vintage C-130 Hercules made for a long and noisy journey to La Aurora Airport in Guatemala City.

After landing in the sweltering humidity, Tina was herded through a processing center where the clothes she was captured in were returned to her along with enough Guatemalan cash to buy a bus ticket downtown.

At one of the Zona Viva boutiques, the clerk remembered Tina and nervously agreed to let her walk out in a new outfit with the promise of "pay later." The owner was out for the day and Tina vowed a prompt return.

Banco Industrial was still open, and the new outfit inspired much more courtesy than the tunnel rat clothes would have. Tina keyed in the appropriate information and was happy to see that Juan de Ochenta's account held more than $3 million. If you couldn't trust your bank, just who could you trust?

A few more minutes of codes, transfer requests and routing information and, bingo, de Ochenta would have to trust her if he ever hoped to see those pesos again.

She also withdrew a sizeable amount of cash in large bills…just the right size packet to fit in her sleek new purse without making an unsightly bulge. Her boots sat snugly in the other, slightly larger, yet stylishly functional shoulder bag.

At the boutique, the obviously relieved clerk was pleased when Tina bought several casual travel outfits and included a substantial cash tip.

"Please come again soon, señorita."

"Whenever I have some banking to do," Tina smiled.

On her way to the hotel, she ducked into an electronics store and bought a brand new cell phone with the built-in camera. She turned down the service plan; she had her own network.

Tina checked into the hotel, put away her purchases and went to the patio restaurant for a late lunch. She selected a table that had a good view of the pool and palm trees for a backdrop, ordered a large, colorful drink and had the waiter take her picture.

The ceviche was tangy, the avocado salad creamy and she treated herself to a coconut custard for dessert. The drink went into the planter bed and the picture went to Señor Rosales, Banamex, Nogales, attention: Juan de Ochenta.

The smiling photo bore the caption: "Do you miss me? Signed, Your Money."

The blind return address would route through the silo, as would Papa's instructions regarding the next fish swimming to port, this time in Puerto Peñasco.

The text message from de Ochenta the next morning apologized for the "misunderstanding" and said he would be happy to see her again.

*Yeah, me and my three million little green friends.*

She selected a pair of pale blue linen cargo pants and matching sleeveless safari shirt for today's travel. As she finished breakfast, a courier envelope arrived with a fresh Mexican passport, a duplicate American version and an Aeronaves de Mexico ticket, first class to Mexico City with a connection north to Hermosillo. Packing was not a problem — her bags were still someplace in Nogales.

In Hermosillo she took a cab through the central square of the old town, then directed the driver to take her to a car dealer.

"Which one, *señorita?* Ford, Chevy, Toyota?"

"*No me hace.*" It didn't matter, and she tipped him well when he dropped her off at the Ford lot. She would be driving from here.

In less than an hour she had picked out a black Expedition that matched the ones Carlos Cabrera had used, no test drive needed thank you, and waved extra cash at the salesman in order to get an "expedited transaction."

"Of course, *señorita*. How much time do you have?"

She pulled out another wad, this time American dollars.

He grinned broadly and handed her the key: "*No problemo, señorita*. I will personally take care of all the papers for you."

Tina took the key and stood up. "Don't you need my name?"

"It's quite alright, *señorita*. I'm sure you have a name. *Mucho gusto en servirle*."

Of course he was happy to provide service at ten thousand bucks an hour. Tina was pleased to see that the Expedition came with a full tank at no extra charge.

Traffic was light on the highway north towards Nogales. At 150 KPH it would take her about two hours. Halfway there, she slowed for a security checkpoint, rolled her window down a few inches and held out a $100 bill for identification. The guard deftly waved her through and snagged the bill in one smooth motion.

Calle Obregón swarmed with early evening nightlife when she reached Nogales. This was a different crowd from the pharmacy, trinket and booze shoppers during the day. Neon signs glowed over the bars and dance clubs that slumbered in daylight.

Tired looking day workers flooded the sidewalks as they walked back from the border after long hours in the distribution centers and warehouses on the American side.

Cab drivers, touts and pimps catcalled to the horde of incoming college boys, construction workers, and crew-cut soldiers and airmen from Fort Huachuca and Davis-Monthan AFB. Music spilled into the street and mixed with the occasional whiff of marijuana.

Tina turned right onto Avenida Reforma and spotted a line of black Expeditions parked in front of Elvira's Bar. She added hers to the queue and stepped inside.

She wasn't the only woman in the place, but she **was** the only one without gaudy makeup and stiletto heels. She spotted Carlos Cabrera and a half dozen of de Ochenta's thugs in the poolroom at the back of the bar.

*The gang's all here.*

José Martinez stood lookout at the archway leading to the tables. Tina couldn't quite use the word "guard" on him.

"Hey, tough guy, remember me?"

He gave her a silent stare. If he was surprised to see her, it didn't show from behind the dark glasses.

She patted his cheek. "That's okay, we can chat later."

Carlos had spotted her and came over to confront her. "Look who's here, our favorite tunnel rat."

"I came back for my suitcases, *cabrón*."

She waved him to a corner. A low partition screened them from the bar, but afforded a view of the entry from the street. Obviously planned that way — furtive transactions could be done quickly.

She stayed between him and the door.

"I assume Señor de Ochenta has discussed his current financial situation with you?"

That put him off balance. His scowl wavered. Tina kept her focus on his hooded eyes as he processed the situation. Finally, he smiled, tried to look "nice."

"Maybe we can start over, be friends, work together, eh?" He moved closer. "Good looking *chiquita* like you. I'd like that."

His parody of a come-on was creepily sinister. Tina kept an eye open for weapons as he moved closer.

When he got within reach, she grabbed his nuts and squeezed.

"Listen, asshole: the Blancos were just for starters. How many other cartel families do you think want to get out of Colombia or Guatemala? Plenty, and at a million a pop, the *Patrón* is going to be pissed if he hears you cost him business."

He tried to clench his teeth and stare her down, but after a couple seconds of Tina's glare — and her crushing grip — he had to settle for a draw. He nodded and she let go. "Okay, *puta,* but I'm watching you."

"*Igualmente, cabrón.* I'm not turning my back on you either. I'll be at de Ochenta's gate at nine tomorrow morning. The first thing I want to see is those suitcases. Some of my favorite undies are in there."

His scowl followed her as she backed away. When she turned toward the door, she gave José a wink.

# Chapter 26

Tina left the Expedition in a bonded lot on the Mexican side, crossed over into the U.S. with her American passport and checked in to Frida's, a classic B&B on Morley Avenue. She took an evening stroll, pretty sure she hadn't been followed back into the American side.

A couple blocks from Frida's, she looked over the railing to where the Morley Tunnel drained into an open channel. The spillway from the Grand Tunnel intersected from the right. Only a month ago she and Luz had been dragged into custody here.

Tina hoped Luz Blanco was okay and enjoying her new life in America. No mother intentionally raised a drug smuggler, but that was one of the highest-paying career paths in Colombia. The flip side: Kidnapping and assassinations were the main occupational hazards.

The last couple of blocks on Morley before the border fence looked like a slice of 1950s Americana. The mix of brick storefronts even included a "Woolworth & Co." façade. Her favorite was Brackers. This was a luxury clothing store with a family history as long as the Goldwater's in Arizona, but stood as an ironic reminder of how much money crossed the border. For all the Americans going into Mexico looking for bargains, many Mexicans did the opposite, coming north to buy luxury goods.

Mama had first brought her here years ago when Papa had been involved in "Commerce Department negotiations" during the pre-NAFTA days. Clothes were beginning to become a problem for Tina with the onset of puberty.

Since the Brackers clientele was primarily wealthy Americans and even wealthier Mexicans, the lower level was packed with designer sportswear. Michelle was indulgent to a fault, and Tina was soon sated with trying on outfits and making the cash register ring.

"Don't stop now, little one. We haven't gone upstairs," Michelle had whispered in French.

"What's upstairs?"

Michelle smiled that little smile that dimpled her cheeks and made her such a mixer at embassy parties. "Why, just a tiny slice of Paris."

Tina's teen horizons had expanded when she had climbed the staircase and seen the gallery of dresses from Chanel, Dior and the rest of the fashion alphabet.

She had settled on a shoulderless, floor length gown, her first "fitted bodice" in a glossy dark blue with tiny white polka dots. She still remembered wearing it to her first embassy party…

…Tonight a pair of black suede pants in the window caught her eye. They looked to be her size and the matching jacket looked elegantly functional. Tomorrow. She checked the door. Open at 9 a.m. Señor de Ochenta would have to wait. She had a little banking to do in the morning, too.

To finish off tonight, she walked across Grand Avenue and up the hill to MacDonalds. A soft vanilla cone provided a "comfort" snack while she hit a phone booth and dialed her secure number for the cutout link to the silo.

"Hello, *hija* where are you?" her father answered on the first ring.

"Hi, Papa, I'm in Nogales. I almost thought about coming to see you tonight, but it was getting late."

"That's okay. I'm in DC doing some fishing for Colombians. Also, we've been getting an updated shopping list from Paris. It looks like Jackson Truong has a couple of black market helicopters in transit."

"What's the ETA?"

"Two weeks at the earliest, depending on the shell game he has to use for transit. More likely three to four weeks.."

"Can you round me up some little fish this week so I can start spreading some cash around?"

"Absolutely. I can set that up immediately. Where would you like the pickup?"

"Puerto Peñasco. I want to script this first travelogue to the last detail. There's no such thing as trust with these bastards, but I want to get them used to handling custom deliveries."

"Understood. Oh, one last detail: Your redhead buddy is now going by the name Sean Adams. He's keeping busy now that Sinn Fein doesn't need his talents. We had a report that he managed a solo meeting in Paris with a low-level al-Qaeda operative from Egypt."

Tina digested that information. "Any guess as to whether he's operating as a buyer or seller."

"All indications are that he's offering to provide anti-aircraft missiles from 'sources' in the U.S. Keep in mind that we're getting these reports second-hand. There aren't enough good guys to go around."

"10-4, Papa. I'd be willing to bet that Sean is thinking he can use Mexican money to take over Jackson Truong's distribution outfit, then use his former IRA ties to go global."

"I wouldn't take that bet honey. Just be careful, okay?"

"Sure, Papa. Let's get this mousetrap built. Or rat trap. And give Mama a hug for me."

The guard in the gatehouse the following morning scowled at her when she rolled down her window. Tina recognized him as one of Carlos' pool hall thugs. She glanced at her watch: 10:30 a.m.

"You're late," he snarled at her.

"I had to do some shopping. Do you also want to chit-chat about the weather and keep Señor de Ochenta waiting, or are you going to open the gate?"

He punched the button and lifted the phone to call ahead. She parked at the top of the circle and gave a wide smile to the white-jacketed attendant who opened her door: "Señor de Ochenta is expecting me."

Nothing had changed in the past month: Jose had door duty, Elvis still sneered at the microphone, blood still trickled from the crown of thorns…oh, the smile was gone from de Ochenta's face.

"You have my money, señorita?"

"First, I think you should apologize for setting me up last time. Or was that Carlos' idea?"

She stared at his lieutenant, who scowled, but made the move she expected: "Señor de Ochenta and I have discussed the unfortunate misunderstanding. It will not happen again."

She looked back at his nominal boss: "Apology accepted. As for your money, it is quite safe in the bank. *My* bank. If you would like to call Señor Rosales at Banamex, he can confirm that I deposited $100,000 just this morning."

The phone call was quick and terse. She imagined Rosales had feared for his life the past week. De Ochenta tried to smile as he hung up.

"*Sí está,* but where's the rest of it?"

"In due time, Juán, and much more if you can prove to my friends in Colómbia that you can be trusted not to double cross their favorite travel agent."

She gave him her sweetest smile. "You already can see that I am a relocation specialist. In addition to relocating people, I can relocate their bank accounts."

"So why the $100,000 deposit?"

"I thought it would be enough for you to take me out tonight for a nice dinner. Just the two of us." She stared pointedly at Carlos.

When she looked back at de Ochenta he was forming one of the warmer smiles Tina had seen from him.

"Since you own El Greco, I was hoping you might close it for the evening so we could have it all to ourselves. I certainly hope Señora de Ochenta wouldn't mind sharing you tonight. You can assure her for me that I am interested only in business. Shall I pick you up here at 7:30?"

She stood, the new black suede pants as comfortable — and conforming — as the Vanson leathers she rode in. Halfway to where José was opening the door for her she turned: "And please be ready on time. You'd hate to keep a lady with $3 million waiting."

She strode out and was happy to see her suitcases on the curb by the Expedition.

That night she relied on black silk instead of leather. The high heels from her suitcase featured a hidden slot for the knife, but de Ochenta did all his frisking with his eyes.

Over dessert she dangled the bait: The Orlando, Flores, Orejuela and Gonzales families. His eyes lit up when he heard the names. The cash from their Colómbian operations totaled into the billions, not millions.

"But there's a problem," she told him.

"Surely, for the right price, we can find a solution to any problem."

"Let us hope so." She licked the last bite of flan from her spoon. "My employers got a mixed report from Señor Blanco about certain difficulties with his trip."

He frowned. "Señorita, please let me apologize again." She couldn't recall him apologizing a first time, but nodded. "This can sometimes be a rough business, and my choices of personnel are somewhat limited."

Limited to thieves, liars and murderers, she thought.

"I will make my own choices," she said. "José will work for me. He seems not to have picked up too many bad habits. Perhaps he can be trained."

He nodded assent.

"In one week I will have my first *cruzeros* ready in Puerto Peñasco. José will help me lead them across the border through the Sasabe corridor."

His eyebrows arched up a notch. "You know this route?"

"I know more than you think. Your people on the other side will finish the delivery to Phoenix. If there are no 'misunderstandings' this time, $1 million of the Flores' retirement fund will be transferred to Banamex, along with $1 million of your own funds which I have kept for safekeeping."

"I can assure you there will be no problems."

"So I fully expect." She stood. "Thank you for dinner, Señor de Ochenta. I hope you don't mind if I don't drive you home, but I have travel arrangements to make."

****

# Chapter 27

Eight days later Tina arrived at de Ochenta's gate unannounced. By now the guard was under standing orders to let her through.

The crossing last night had gone smoothly and José had lost some of his surly edge. The only hint of possible trouble had been when Carlos had showed up in one of the Expeditions at the pickup point. It was now obvious to Tina that he was playing both sides of the fence, probably in league with Jackson Truong and Sean Adams.

So much the better; it verified that she was on the right trail.

Tina had picked José as her attaché because he seemed to be the least dangerous of de Ochenta's thugs. Besides, he wasn't too tough on her eyes and sometimes even seemed smarter than he looked.

When she got to de Ochenta's office, José was at the door, as usual, but the rest of the entourage was gone.

"Señorita, what a pleasant surprise," de Ochenta said, standing up from his throne behind the desk. It was obvious to her that he had gotten a call from Señor Rosales at Banamex that morning.

"Forgive me for seeming in a hurry, Señor, but I must speak to you in private."

He nodded to José, who at least did not protest as he went outside and shut the door behind him.

"Has there been a problem, Señorita?"

She still refused to let him call her by her first name.

"No, more like an opportunity," she smiled, getting ready to bait the hook. "My employers are very happy with your organization's recent performance. We have a rather urgent situation that we would like to discuss with you, but it would involve a personal meeting at a place of their choosing."

He frowned, sat back down in his chair. She gave him couple seconds to stew, then purred: "What's the matter, Juán? I think you should trust me by now."

He looked sullen and unconvinced. "What do you want from me?"

"First, to stop worrying. Bring a gun if it makes you feel safer."

That seemed to convince him. He stood, opened his center drawer, picked up a Glock and looked at her. She gave him her best "contented Buddha" look. He nodded to himself, the pendulum of decision slowly ticking. Finally he put the gun away, closed the drawer and came around the desk.

"Where are we going?"

"For a little ride," she smiled. "And I won't even blindfold you."

She stopped at the gate on the way out and let the guard see that de Ochenta was a willing passenger. As she drove through the *maquíladora* section, she pointed to the glove box: "There's something in there you'll need."

He opened the door to find a folder, the usual string closure and wax seal affixed to it. He broke the seal, lifted the flap, pulled out a weathered looking American passport.

"Go ahead, open it." She knew what it would contain: a recent photo of him lifted from a family birthday a year ago, plenty of stamps to give the passport a well traveled look, and the name "Juan Toledo."

His smile was mixed with curiosity.

As he continued to stare at the passport, she said: "I make pretty good travel arrangements, don't I Juan?"

"So where are you taking me?"

"For dinner across the border to meet your new friend."

He slipped the passport into his shirt pocket. "I hope this isn't total bullshit."

Don't worry, she thought, you haven't seen the show yet.

She wheeled the Expedition expertly through the warehouses and factories. Most Americans came south to Nogales on the Arizona side and saw a tiny town of a handful more than 20,000 people. A couple hours of shopping in the first few blocks of "Mexico" and they were done, not realizing that a small metropolis of more than half a million people stretched into the hills to the south.

She parked the Expedition in the bonded lot and led de Ochenta to the easternmost pedestrian gate. This was away from the tourist section and had shorter lines, mostly day workers crossing to the transshipment warehouses on the American side.

"This beats slogging through a tunnel or walking hours across the desert, don't you think, Juan?"

De Ochenta looked a little nervous, but then relieved when the Customs agent glanced at their passports and waved them through. Tina gave him a ya'at'eeh nod as she followed de Ochenta out the gate, then led him down Morley Avenue and in the front door of Brackers.

"Do you need a jacket or anything?" Tina asked. "Actually, I'd suggest a nice Stetson — change your look a little."

He understood that logic and let her pick a gray one that made him look like just another ranch hand. When she led him out the back door, he seemed a little surprised to see another black Expedition sitting by the curb.

As they drove north out of town, Tina set the hook a little deeper: "You like Expeditions, too, don't you? I just wanted you to see how well I'm spending the money my *patróns* entrust to me."

"These are the same families you have mentioned to me before?"

"Aha, you guessed. Yes, those families and more." She put on her most businesslike look. "The man you are going to meet has worked with many of these people as they worked very hard to gather money, a lot of money. They worked hard for this money and now they expect it to work hard for them."

The sun was sinking low to her left as she merged onto Interstate 19. The warehouse and transshipment yards of Rio Rico covered the Santa Cruz River plain to their right, while "resort" homes dotted the hillsides to their left.

She stayed in the right lane; the trucks were going plenty fast for her.

All the freeway south of Tucson was marked in kilometers, so at KM 29, less than 20 miles north of Nogales, she exited toward Tumacacori Mission. This remnant of Padre Kino's northward march was not much more than an adobe shell along the river, nothing like the jewel of the desert: San Xavier del Bac in Tucson, where Nez met Estrella decades ago.

De Ochenta watched the mission out his window, making a small sign of the cross as they passed. This surprised Tina a little, but she had already tapped Carlos Calderón as the brains, and evil, of the group.

A half-mile down on the right, she pulled in to the dirt parking lot of Wisdoms, an old café that once sat on the highway, but had been left behind when the Interstate was built. She led de Ochenta in past the array of antique tack, farm hardware and photos. In the back corner sat the man she had brought de Ochenta to meet.

As Papa stood up, Tina said, "Señor de Ochenta, please meet Señor Toledo."

De Ochenta thought for a second, tapped the passport in his pocket and laughed. Both men nodded but did not shake hands.

Over a dinner of Mexican specialties that ensured that tourists who found Wisdom's off the beaten path were certain to return, the two men discussed logistics, schedules and money. Tina skipped the dinner and ordered a fruit burrito with ice cream, the specialty that made her keep coming back.

"One more thing," Papa said. "I have spent much money and bought the allegiance of many government officials to make retirement plans for my patrons. The most secure arrangements must be arranged for the third crossing. It will be Señor Orejuela himself."

De Ochenta's eyes widened. Orejuela's wealth was matched only by the ruthless trail of bodies he had left behind in Colómbia.

Papa set the hook even deeper: "Señor Orejuela's health has not been as good as it could be lately." A rival's assassination attempt had left Orejuela with a limp and the rival with a new headstone. "Señor Orejuela insists on dealing with *El Negro* for transportation by helicopter."

De Ochenta's eyes opened even wider at the mention of Jackson Truong. A second later, they narrowed suspiciously: "You know about this man?"

"Certainly," Papa said, not missing a beat. "My clients have steered many lucrative negotiations his way. Señorita Corazón here has even done some banking transactions for him."

De Ochenta was hooked. When they stood to leave, he held out his hand to Papa. He shook it.

When they returned to Nogales, Tina let de Ochenta out of the car a block from the border. He would have no trouble crossing the border *out* of the U.S.

****

# Chapter 28

She told José she had a special scouting assignment for him, that it would involve some walking. "Think of it as a campout. I'll bring the food."

He gave her his sternest scowl, but relented after checking with de Ochenta. Tina drove, the Expedition loaded with gear, her two suitcases and a hidden selection of more "toys."

A network of dirt roads paralleled the border west of Nogales. Despite her best efforts at casual conversation, José stayed glum and mum. By the time they reached Sasabe, he was staring away from her out the window.

They began climbing, the road a little scarcer, much more rugged.

"Do you know the name of these mountains?" she asked as the Expedition crawled toward the ridgeline.

He shrugged her off, staring out the window with a determination that she found more admirable than annoying. "No."

She knew. The Pozo Verde Mountains were a little tail at the bottom of the Baboquivaris. To the north and west, they would be crossing the border into her maze.

Darkness would be soon and absolute, so she found the first convenient flat spot after they hit the downward slope.

She opened the tailgate and took out the first load of gear to set up camp. When she set it down, she turned and found herself staring at José with a gun. He waved her around against the side of the truck and poked the gun into her ribs. It was a Glock and she knew it would only need one bullet to send her to forever.

"Your stories don't add up so I need to sort a few things out. Let's start with who the hell are you?"

"You know who I am: Valentina Corazón from Quetzaltenango, Guatemala."

"That's bullshit and so is the accent. I saw your ears perk up when that group of Chinos went through. They don't speak a lot of Chinese in Guatemala. I've also noticed how you pretend you're doing something, but you're always listening to stuff in the background. I think you're a spy."

Mutely, she shook her head, but her nerves kept him in edgy focus.

He dug the gun into her ribs, staring at her. "I also got a lot of crap from Carlos when I let you trot off with Señor de Ochenta last week."

He backed up half a step, arm extended, the gun still locked to her ribs, pointing at her heart. "I'm not going to let some coyote bitch double cross me. One of my friends was already killed, so I don't trust anybody."

She swallowed her shock. "You knew Ruben?"

The gun pressed harder; he glared at her through slits for eyes. "How do you know his name?"

"I not only know his name, I knew *him*. We went to school together."

"Where?" He spat to the left, his eyes not moving. "Fucking Guatemala?"

There was only one hope — that Ruben had for some reason trusted José and that she could, too. The door was open an inch. She had no other choice; the gun was too close, her knife too far. The situation had a precarious balance, but she had to believe in *hozho,* the Middle Way, grasp for the center.

"No, not Guatemala. I knew him from when we went to Annapolis."

The gun was still at her ribs, but not pressing quite as hard. "How do you know he went there? He could have told you that under torture. Maybe you killed him yourself."

"I knew Ruben. We went through POW training together later in the Marines. He wouldn't talk."

José stared mutely, his eyes locked with hers. The silence stretched in the still desert twilight.

Tina was running out of time. She tried the deepest breath she could squeeze into her lungs, conscious of the steel barrel holding her locked against the truck.

"Listen to me," she said. "Let's make this a conversation. I tell you everything I know. You tell me what you know. If it doesn't add up, then you can kill me."

A trace of a smile softened his lips. He relaxed infinitesimally. "I do have the gun, don't I?"

That instant was all it took. Tina twisted the Glock out of his hand and had it pointed at his forehead while his question mark still hung in the air.

"My turn," she said, circling around, waving him up against the truck. He raised his hands slowly without being told. "Start with telling me who killed Ruben."

"I don't know."

She held the pistol with both hands, completely still, her heartbeat returning to double digits.

"I might believe that. Maybe we try something now. I tell you my story, you tell me yours. If we find something we both believe, we'll call that the truth."

He nodded.

"You first."

"It started with my father," he said. "He was the police chief in Sasabe. All he wanted to do was keep the narco traffickers under control so the tourists could roll south to Puerto Peñasco. His brother had a boat there and we would go every month to get shrimp."

He took a deep breath. "It was ten years ago. I came home from school and saw blood everywhere. He and my mother were both dead. His head was gone; it ended up tossed on the steps of the police station as a warning. Some federal guys came and helped me move to Hermosillo so I could finish school. When I got out, I joined the **Federales**. After a couple years, everything just kept getting worse. When they asked me if I wanted to try to get inside de Ochenta's gang, I agreed."

"How did you find out who Ruben really was?"

"He told me. He had been working his way in for about three years, but then he found something coming that was too big for him. I don't know how he found out who I really worked for, but he had his suspicions…just like I had my suspicions about you."

Tina lowered the Glock, but kept her grip on it. "Go on."

"Like I said, it was big. There's money and drugs and people all the time, but now there was so much money that it was going for guns, rockets too, and he thought maybe even a helicopter. He was sending signals but was locked 176inside so deep he couldn't get out. Except the wrong way."

She gave him back the pistol, moved around beside him, leaned against the truck and stared into the night, suddenly drained.

"Mexico has its problems, same as you, mostly worse," he said. "We have a million illegal immigrants coming north from Central America every year, and probably a third of those try to get all the way into the United States.

"The Mexicans who can find a job here in the *maquiladoras* are the lucky ones. They come in dirt poor from the countryside, happy to work for cheap wages and see all that nice, new stuff loaded on trucks heading north across the border. But because of the rules, they can't even buy any of the stuff they make."

He turned, went to the tailgate and lifted a sleeping bag out of the truck. "They want a better life for their families, so they risk everything to go north, look for a better job. It's the American way, no?"

She smiled, reached in for the other sleeping bag. When they had eaten some sandwiches and settled into their bags, Tina gazed at the night sky, littered with stars. "Your turn for the next question."

He took a deep breath. "You and Ruben, were you...?"

"I don't have to answer that one, but no, we were friends. Really good friends. And cousins."

As she stared into space, she remembered the night in another desert when Ruben had flown a chopper along the deck to yank her out of Kuwait City before "shock and awe" descended on Saddam Hussein's troops.

Drifting into dream, she remembered the dark night, weaving her way through the streets emptied by curfew and sporadic gunfire. She hadn't needed to stick to the shadows — blackness ruled the night.

In her burqa, she slipped like a ghost past the scattered patrols and made her way out of the city into the sandy flats. After a good half hour of walking she pulled her watch from a fold of cloth and slipped it onto her wrist: almost midnight.

From another fold of cloth she pulled what looked to be a small cassette player, complete with a tape printed in Arabic. She pulled the tape out and tossed it away, opened the battery compartment, pulled out the two AA-size batteries, kept them, and flipped a small switch hidden on the side of the battery compartment.

The radio beacon did its job quickly. Within ten minutes she heard the characteristic thumping noise of helicopter blades that had led to the term "chopper." She pulled the burqa off over her head and neatly arranged it in a pile. Underneath, she was wearing black woolen pants and a sweater befitting a wealthy Kuwaiti woman — complete with Parisian labels — camouflage would have marked her right away as a spy.

A thumbnail slipped under the cap of a battery, pried it open and a blaze of phosphorous erupted from the mini-flare. She tossed it onto the burqa, followed it with the second "battery" and flipped another hidden switch on the cassette player.

The "on" light was a small laser, but enough to guide Ruben right to the impromptu landing zone.

The black Apache was on the ground for only a second before Tina was crawling into the front seat.

"*Buenas noches, Tausongatina. Ni a ni mea e fai?*" Ruben's "Where are you heading?" in Samoan was in her earphones just as she clamped the canopy latch and spotted one of Saddam's patrols racing toward them — probably alerted by the flaming burqa.

"Let's just get out of here!" she hollered as Ruben throttled up and the Apache leapt forward and twisted away from the first tracers fired at them by the patrol.

We probably saved those bastards' lives, she thought, as Ruben circled the helicopter out across the trackless dark. Minutes from now, the first wave of aerial attacks would be following the beacons she had set in the past few days. Tons of munitions would be honing in on the electronic targets she had installed right under the noses of the Iraqi garrisons.

The patrol that had come racing after her would, if they were lucky, watch the fireworks from a distance and someday tell their grandchildren how they had bravely chased away a helicopter of the attacking infidels.

The last memory before sleep overtook her was of how Ruben had let her take the controls and follow the flight path out to the waiting carrier for her debriefing. If her Sea Knight cargo chopper was like steering a limo, this Apache was a Ferrari…with a lot of firepower.

****

# Chapter 29

This was going to be an overland excursion, but only partly. Tina was determined to make the contact, see the coyotes who would be driving the vehicles to the rendezvous and personally wave around some money — cash and the bigger electronicly transferred jackpot that could only be triggered by greed.

Human nature had yet to disappoint her when it came to greed. Buddha hit the target in the bullseye when he said the root of suffering is desire.

Her desire now was an ever-growing quest for revenge, but she figured the Middle Way wasn't a straight line and the *hozho* — her Navajo culture of "balance" — could tip one way or the other.

If she got a chance to kick some ass, she was ready.

José was much more companionable these days. She counted on him as an ally now, but didn't go so far as to rely.

They scouted the walking part of the crossing: the route would be into the Tohono O'odham reservation, then by helicopter up to a van southwest of Casa Grande — the stretch of desert where Tina had tracked the semi with explosive results.

The landing zone looked familiar, but Tina was happy to see that most of Black Eagle's tire prints had faded away.

She steered José away from her electronic friends, even though they were mostly invisible, and waved to a patch of shade under a mesquite tree for a break before beginning the walk back.

Something about the night she had been dumped in the tunnel still bothered her, so she probed José for any clue he could provide, either knowingly or through ignorance: "You were there when we took the Blanco family across, but what was Carlos doing in the pickup wagon with the phony Border Patrol guys?"

"He said he was making sure you didn't screw up the crossing."

"So he screwed it up and made sure we got captured, then he could look like a hero by springing the Blancos and pinning it on me."

"And skimming some of the cash for himself."

"Is he really working for Señor de Ochenta or is he in with the Americans?"

José gave her a sidelong look, spat at the ground as if getting rid of a bad taste. "Carlos works for himself. He was the main henchman of de Ochenta's father, and would have taken over, but he got unlucky and was out of town when the old man got killed."

"He was going to take over from the family? What stopped him?"

"Ruben was there. Ruben helped de Ochenta hold together enough of his organization that Carlos was outgunned when he got back, so he had to step back into the organization and bide his time."

"Until he could kill Ruben."

"Maybe, but I'm not sure. He never said anything about that, but he told de Ochenta that Ruben was double crossing us. Carlos found some electronic spy gizmos and told de Ochenta he went looking for Ruben, but that Ruben had split across the border."

"So how did you hear that Ruben was dead?

"Email. Whoever shot him took a video of his head sitting on the ground and sent it to us."

Tina fought back a retch. Papa had spared her this detail. She put her head between her knees and took a deep breath. Her right hand ran across the inseam of her boot, fingered the knife.

José laid his arm across her shoulder. The silence of the desert witnessed the bond she now felt growing: her, José and the spirit Ruben left behind.

Tina raised her head, took a deep breath and gave José a pat on his thigh. "Thanks, I'm better."

In the distance the sun glinted off the observatories atop Kitt Peak. Looming closer stood Baboquivari – the navel of the world – where I'itoi brought the first people up from the underworld and gave them *Himdag,* the guidelines of how to live in balance with the world.

Restoring balance to this violent corner would be tough.

****

# Chapter 30

Tina was not surprised to see Carlos Cabrera at the pickup point later that week. The night crossing had been mild; early fall temperatures dropping into the 70s made the walk passable. The group from the Flores family had been teens to young adults, mobile and relieved that their new life was about to begin.

Having plenty of drug money to buy passage helped.

The black Expedition pulled out of the shadows right at midnight. Carlos got out of the passenger side and started barking orders to the Floreses to get into the back seat and cargo bay.

The driver got out to collect the two backpacks full of cash Tina and José were carrying. As he emerged through the darkness, clad in camouflage, she spotted his red hair a second before he recognized her.

"Here's your money, Sean." She threw the backpack at his feet.

The cash landed on his boot, almost tripping him. He was even more surprised when he looked at her: "How the fuck you know my name? Hey — you're that bitch that broke my nose!"

"Come here and I'll break it again."

He started toward her, but José stepped between them, thrusting his backpack against the Irishman's camo jacket: "Don't mess with the cash machine, *señor.*"

Carlos also joined the fray, pulling the redhead back by his shoulder: "I see you've met our *puta* banker girl. Come on, let's get out of here before 'break time' is over in the sector." He grabbed the second backpack from José.

Sean put his hand to the bridge of his nose, rubbed its crooked contour and picked up the other bag: "You and I have a score to settle."

"You don't know the half of it, carrot top."

The juvenile nickname brought one more snarl from him as he turned away. He scattered gravel as he gunned the truck and headed north to the next rendezvous on the Flores' itinerary.

Tina looked at José, rubbed her nose and laughed in relief as the leftover adrenaline filtered through her blood.

"I don't get it," he said. "Are you trying to piss him off on purpose?"

"Sure. That testosterone will cloud his thinking, plus I want them to gang up on us. That will bring out the big dog."

"What loco idea are you talking about?"

She told him about Jackson Truong – "El Negro" – and her plan to snare him. Not the details, of course, that much knowledge could get them both killed.

"No sirve – it won't work. They're not going to buy it."

"They will the way I sell it."

"I still think you're loco."

"Good. I also want you pissed off about tonight so you can convince de Ochenta that you want no part of it."

"Porqué?"

On the walk back she translated the tale about Br'er Fox and Br'er Rabbit and the concept of the briar patch. She wanted José thrown deep inside it.

\*\*\*\*

# Chapter 31

Tina strode into Señor de Ochenta's office right on time the next afternoon, barely glanced at José, gave Carlos her best sneer, pulled a bank deposit receipt from her purse and laid it on de Ochenta's desk.

He picked it up, smiled at the balance and folded it into his shirt pocket. He was totally ill equipped for this line of work, she thought, and would probably end up suffering the same fate as his father. *Et tu, Brute?*

"Don't look so pleased. That might be the last deposit I make with your two-bit organization."

His mouth dropped open and he stood up, but no words came.

"Tell him what happened last night, Carlos."

"Don't get pushy, bitch. We held up our end of the transfer. You pissed on the Americans. That's not our problem."

"Well you should make it your problem — get another subcontractor on the other end if that's what it takes to do the job right. And he's Irish, not American"

She turned to José: "How about you, junior, tell Señor de Ochenta about the warm welcome we got."

"*Hija de puta,*" he spat back. "It's *cagada, Patrón.* Are we going to let this slut push us around just because she carries the money? Tell the Colombians to send us a different errand girl."

His performance was pretty convincing. Tina smiled at him: "*Pobrecito*…I don't think you want to tell Señor Orejuela much of anything. I think you *listen* to Señor Orejuela.."

"I don't give a shit." He walked past her to the edge of de Ochenta's desk. "I'm sick of her crap, *Patrón.* How about let somebody else carry her around?"

Tina noticed Carlos' smirk. José was definitely earning bad-guy points as per her plan.

De Ochenta, also as predicted, backed away from what for him would be giving up easy cash: "No, José. Señorita Corazón assured me in advance that she would put you all through some rigorous tests to make sure she was not left stranded as she was in the tunnel." He gave Tina a smarmy smile. "I assure you, Señorita, I will have my men make certain that you and Señor Orejuela are warmly welcomed."

Tina turned to Carlos: "Let the redhead know there are no hard feelings, okay? But he still better not get near me."

*Please don't throw me into that briar patch.*

The next night's crossing didn't go as planned. Not as Tina told them it was planned, that is.

She stayed in Puerto Peñasco with Señor Orejuela and sent José to the rendezvous empty-handed, except for half the cash and a note with assurances that there would be a bonus the following night, sorry for the delay. Orejuela was a tired man of seven decades who looked worse for wear than Grandfather Nez, despite Nez' additional decade. He was a pretty good chess player, however, and as they sat on the patio of his hotel room looking out at Bahia de California, he listened carefully at Tina scripted the role he was to play at the helicopter pickup the following night.

When José returned, she went downstairs to his room and grilled him: Yes, they were pissed, but, yes, the cash calmed them down. Yes, the helicopter was on time.

"How many seats?"

"Five," he told her and sketched it out on the pad she gave him. No, no numbers on the tail, he said.

It matched Papa's description of the Eurocopter EC 120B that Jackson Truong had been looking at in Paris. It was no Apache, but without the heavy armor plates, it was a fast and maneuverable rig.

The most important detail from José: Yes, they had taken the entire backpack along with the cash. Tina smiled as she thought of the electronic circuitry sewn into the lining with such artistry that it looked like part of the stitching. The neck of the noose began to close.

The final detail of the evening: She showed him the backpack for the next night. Lifting out one stack of bills, she tapped the bottom. "Half a kilo of *plastica*."

She closed the top of the pack, rolled it over and showed him the switch built into the buckle on the bottom of the strap. "*Cinco minutos*. Make sure you're right up to the helicopter door when you switch it on, then get back to the car while I'm helping Señor Orejuela hobble over to the chopper."

"Why hobble?"

"Because it's in the script."

She stood to go and he caught her elbow. Turning to him, she patted his cheek — tenderly this time.

He gently reeled her elbow to him: "*Tén quidado*. Be careful."

She took the step to complete her part of the hug: "I will *caro*, but Ruben was careful, too."

His half of the hug became an embrace. She completed it.

They left just after noon the next day. There would be a couple hours of driving northeast from the beach to get to the remote desert south of Sasabe. In this area, the elaborate upward reaches of the Organ Pipe cactis ruled the rocks.

Unlike the Saguaros with their humanoid shapes, many of whom looked like football referees signaling a touchdown, the Organ Pipes sprouted dozens of arms directly up from the ground, looking much like, well, a church organ.

Their pace slowed as the sun impaled itself on the cactus arms, then dropped below the horizon.

José was well-practiced at crawling over rough terrain in the Expedition. The radio, while not as advanced as what Tina had on Black Eagle, scanned the Border Patrol spectrum.

Sean had guaranteed, though, that patrols from this sector would be diverted to the area southwest of Sells. A marijuana-loaded truck bouncing through the desert was a good decoy.

She figured drug runners alone could provide an unlimited supply of bad guys unless the U.S. changed its policy to regulation instead of criminalization. But that domino was unlikely to fall. The prison-for-profit industry, a.k.a. "corrections," was making billions, so "tough on crime" as a sales tool was here to stay.

As the first glimpse of Baboquivari rose in the darkness, Tina quizzed Señor Orejuela one last time about his performance.

"Yó entiendo." He understood. She also understood that this was his only way out of the maze of drugs, money and death that had become his life.

José pulled into a brushy thicket a hundred meters from the pickup zone. Now they would wait. Tina made an excuse about using one of the bushes and got out of the truck and circled around the landing zone. An occasional bat swooped down to snag bugs stirred up by her walking.

Her electronic friends were all scattered right where she had carefully placed them weeks ago. She had almost completed the loop when the faint thumping of the helicopter came into earshot. She checked her watch: ten minutes behind schedule. She reached down and squeezed the switch in the lining of her left boot. In the distance a lone coyote howled.

She climbed back into the rig and José drove ahead and parked on the edge of the circle, lights on to illuminate the landing zone. The chopper faced them as it landed, Sean Adams at the controls. Next to him, Jackson Truong looked bigger than Tina had imagined.

He stepped out the door, followed by Carlos. Tina walked right up to Truong, her eyes at about his shoulder level. He wore round wire-rim glasses, his chocolate skin was flecked with dark moles and his short hair salted with white.

"You're late," she said.

"You too, by about a day."

"It couldn't be helped," she waved toward the car. Señor Orejuela was leaning against the door, bent over slightly. Good, she thought, not overplaying it too much. José was lifting the backpack from the cargo bay.

She turned back to Truong and Carlos, pointed to Orejuela: "You guys help me bring the old man over while Junior loads the money."

Jackson's lips twitched up at the mention of cash: "I see you brought a bigger bag."

Tina smiled sweetly at him. *If only you knew, asshole.*

While they walked over to the station wagon, she kept her eye on the helicopter. Sean took the bag from José and placed it behind his seat. The rotor blades had idled to a stop and the redhead flipped her the bird. She smiled and gave him a wave.

"*Como esta, Viejo?*" Carlos said, mocking the old man when they got to the car.

"That's Señor Viejo, to you, punk," Orejuela told him.

"Quit being a tough guy and help him to the chopper," Tina ordered Carlos.

José was almost back to the car when tear gas started billowing from behind the pilot seat of the helicopter. It was supposed to drive the occupants out of the cabin, but instead Sean grabbed the fire extinguisher and began spraying the backpack.

Wrong reaction, Tina thought. Two seconds later the copter exploded in flames.

"*Cabrones!*" Carlos shouted and pulled a gun. He wheeled toward José and as he began to lift the barrel, Tina pushed Truong into him, but the shot split the night and José spun to the ground.

Carlos was turning back toward her, the gun barrel coming up to eye level when his forehead exploded in red. The shot had come from her right, and as Tina turned, Señor Orejuela said, "Not bad for a Viejo, *como no señorita?*" He proudly displayed a chrome derringer.

But he shouldn't have taken his eyes off "El Negro." Truong fired twice from the ground with Carlos' pistol, and Orejuela collapsed against the car, blood streaming from his chest. Truong turned the gun on her. Tina could see it was a Glock, a very popular model in the thousands of gun shops that dotted the border from California through Texas.

"What the fuck are you doing?" he hissed at her. "Now I have to kill you and drive this piece of shit car back through the desert."

Tina strained her ears against the night, heard only silence. This was not at all like the plan. The cavalry was supposed to be flying to her rescue, but all she had were words against bullets.

She spoke to him in Vietnamese: "You can't kill me; we might be cousins. Besides, there's still more money wanting to buy a seat on your airline. You can always get another helicopter."

"Who the fuck are you?" he replied in kind, waving the gun barrel to signal her to kneel. "You convince me a Vietnamese bitch can wind up pushing money in Colombia, I let you live. Put your hands behind your back."

"We're on the same side, remember? It's who's left standing with the money that wins," she said as she slipped to her knees, hands behind her back.

"Wrong answer," he switched back to English. "The last time someone tried that one on me, I had to kill the Samoan bastard."

Tina reached for the knife, pissed, her anger over-riding the instinct for self-preservation. Adrenaline magnified her swiftness as she lunged upward, slashing the razor-honed blade in the dark...Saddam's soldiers had come after her in the dark in Kuwait. Two followed her into a small side street, she emerged alone on the other end...

Only the element of surprise kept her alive. The shock of the first knife thrust bent Truong over, his instinctive trigger pull sending the shot over the roof of the car. Her left fist came around hard on his temple sending him to the ground, the gun spinning away.

She grabbed the Glock and rolled Truong over. If he was lucky, he would live to tell more lies.

From the bushes, Tina heard a groan; It was José!

As she ran to him, the reverberation of two choppers echoed in the air from Baboquivari.

José tried to push himself up, grabbed at his thigh. "Shit, what happened?" When he saw Tina coming toward him he smiled.

She smiled back: "Don't worry, Junior, I'll tell you all about the shootout. You did great."

Her kiss urged him to lie back down. A spotlight from the sky swept the sand as the flames from the first helicopter subsided.

\*\*\*\*

# Chapter 32

Three weeks later, after many debriefings and interrogations, usually with Papa present, Tina left to put the last personal piece of the mission to rest. Before she checked out from the silo she stopped at José's room, gave him a big kiss and congratulated him on his new job.

He would make a great Good Guy. He had already proven he was someone she could trust. Truong would never be trusted, but at least he would cooperate, in custody, tracking the arms network upstream towards terror groups worldwide. The secure cell in the silo was much preferable to a federal prison.

As the Samoa Air jetliner descended from the clouds over Tutuila Island, Tina saw Pago Pago nestled against the crescent of harbor. The island was like a huge chunk of jade, the volcanic outcroppings covered in dense vegetation that glowed a bright green against the blue of the Pacific.

At the airport, she boarded a trolley that wound its way from the summit of the ridge down to Pago Pago harbor spotted with boats. The curved shoreline was the result of a collapsed volcano and the sheer ridges that ringed the water were steeper, and greener, than anything Tina had ever seen.

She took a small open-air cab along the coastline to Fagatogo, where she climbed up a zig-zag of steps to a cliffside shanty overlooking the harbor. In this neighborhood, the terrain was nothing but cliff and harbor.

Standing on the porch with a big smile was Ruben's mother Petania Mataia Gonzalez, a graying woman about the same age as Mama Michelle, but her face and body rounded by the Samoan side of her family. Her hugs were strong.

"Come sit and I'll make you some coffee," Petania said, her hospitality and twinkling eyes containing strong Navajo traces. She told Tina many stories of Ruben's childhood and the family's history on the island.

Although the shanty had no phone, it seemed like every ten minutes another cousin or uncle of Ruben's would show up. Petania was like a den mother: "This is one of the Toledo-Gonzales boys," or "This is Moon Dog Mataia." Tina feasted her ears on vowels.

After a jet-lagged sleep, Tina rode another cab with Petania into the jungle to a small village where she met many more cousins and enjoyed a traditional Samoan *fa'alavelaves* or feast.

The open-air ramadas in the park alongside the cemetery reminded Tina of the brush arbors of Navajoland, except for the palm frond roofing. She was fascinated by the flying foxes that leapt through the trees, wary of the humans but not too proud to jump down for a snack thrown to the edge of the clearing by the children.

When the many introductions and courses of tropical delicacies were done, Tina addressed the group and thanked them for the warm welcome.

"You have let me enter your family and I will keep you in my heart as I travel the path of life. I know we all wish Ruben could be here." Then in her rudimentary Samoan: *"Ona alu ai lea 'o le tamaloa, se a se mea e fai."*

To a smattering of applause and not a few wiped eyes, she presented Petania with a black velvet box. Brushing back a tear, Ruben's mother opened it to see a purple ribbon with a gold medallion, emblazoned with an eagle on one side, and on the other a single word: "Valor."

Many more stories were traded before a late afternoon rain shower and a spectacular rainbow drew the curtain on the day.

In the morning Tina took a cab and returned to the cemetery alone.

In the corner where the veterans and war dead were memorialized, Ruben's stone of black lava stood at the cliff edge looking out over the wide sweep of the ocean below.

She had helped make the arrangements, and as she knelt down and opened her backpack, Tina quickly spotted the threaded mount embedded in the lava monolith.

She lifted a bundle wrapped in a small Navajo blanket — a tiny tapestry of three corn maidens she had woven as a girl first learning the craft. She carefully unrolled the contents onto the grass. The bronze of the plaque glowed under the tropical sun. Tina licked a tear that had crawled down her cheek, took a deep breath and carefully threaded the mounting bolt into the stone, turning until it was solidly screwed into place with the figure of I'itoi at the top. Above the winding circular maze was the name:

**Ruben Mataia Gonzalez**
**1965-1999**
**Annapolis Class of 1986**

Curving below the maze was the epitaph Tina had spoken to Ruben's family the night before: *"Ona alu ai lea 'o le tamaloa, se a se mea e fai."*

**A man who did what needed to be done.**

######

**About the author:**
Phil Baechler is an inventor, journalist, artist and longtime Arizona resident.

You can email Phil at philbaechler@gmail.com

**\*\*\*\***

**Next:** In the aftermath of September 11, 2001, Jackson Truong's links to terror groups, including Al Qaeda and Osama Bin Laden, may provide a clue to trapping weapons traffickers. Worse, one of Tina's electronic tracking beacons has been traced to Los Alamos, New Mexico, raising the specter of a possible theft of nuclear materials. Watch for *Toxic Trail,* coming in 2017.